Brave

WENDY CONSTANCE

From the Chicken House

Wendy Constance brilliantly rips us back in time to a world of the super-tough, where young and old alike survive or get eaten by something very scary. Here, sabretooth cats rub hairy shoulders with mammoths – but actually, in the end, a bit of kindness goes much further than our brave-hearted boy and skilful girl can ever have imagined. And I'm going to try that recipe for snake kebabs myself . . .

Barry Cunningham
Publisher

Brave

WENDY CONSTANCE

Chicken House

2 PALMER STREET, FROME, SOMERSET BA11 1DS

Text © Wendy Constance 2014
Inside illustrations © Wendy Constance 2014

First published in Great Britain in 2014
The Chicken House
2 Palmer Street
Frome, Somerset, BA11 1DS
United Kingdom
www.doublecluck.com

Cover and interior design by Steve Wells
Cover illustrations by Steve Rawlings
Typeset by Dorchester Typesetting Group Ltd
Printed and bound in Great Britain by CPI Group (UK) Ltd, Croydon, CR0 4YY

The paper used in this Chicken House book is made from wood grown in sustainable forests.

1 3 5 7 9 10 8 6 4 2

British Library Cataloguing in Publication data available.

ISBN 978-1-909489-05-9
eISBN 978-1-909489-52-3

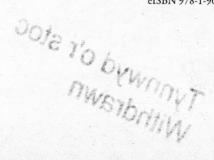

To SP

Route of Wild Horse's and Blue Bird's Journey

KEY

M mountains
hills
forest
— river

Great River

Falling River

Big (Red) River

Blackwater Lake

Great Plains

Ravine

Land of Hills

Sacred Rock

start

Sea

end

CHAPTER ONE

WILD HORSE

This was the kill that Wild Horse yearned for. *Father will be proud of me again*, he thought. The vision of Bear Face holding up the tusks, showing them to the rest of the tribe around the evening fire, twisted about him. It was this picture in his mind that made him cross the river, though he knew it was dangerous to approach such a large animal on his own. One swipe with that trunk would break his back.

There was no time to remove his leggings and moccasins. The cold water curled round his legs as a bitter breeze stung his nostrils. At least he was downwind, his own scent carried away from his prey. Barely aware of the whoosh of the river, the rustling of the reeds, the caws and carks of the birds, his own breathing, Wild Horse gripped his spear tightly. He climbed up the riverbank, keeping his gaze on the danger he was about to face.

The mammoth stood nearly twice as tall as him, those prized tusks almost as long as his own body. It munched the scrubland as he edged forward.

He had to get near enough to thrust his spear-point deep into the throat, piercing the thick matted hair. The mammoth would not get far with such a fatal wound. Then he would chase it and finish the kill with his newly sharpened stone knife. He wished he had another spear – if he missed his target he would be crushed by the beast, or hurled back across the river.

Too late to worry. He was close now, so close that he gagged at the reek of rancid grass surging from the mouth of his prey. The mammoth looked up, and Wild Horse lunged. He hurled his spear as hard as he could.

The mammoth flicked away the weapon with its trunk.

And Wild Horse had no idea what to do next.

The creature stood in front of him, still chewing, sturdy as one of the rocks that punched its way out of the earth. A rock with eyes, watching him. A rock blocking his way to the safety of the woodland beyond the river. A rock with long curved tusks which could thrust his body into the sky or rip him apart. But hadn't – yet.

It was a young bull, not quite full-grown, probably abandoned by the herd when its mother had a new calf. It was a grass-eater so it didn't need to kill him for food, and if he was the first human it had seen it would not know to fear him.

But Wild Horse had threatened it. What would it do now? He knew he must not show his fear. He had to stay calm and still.

As the son of a chief, Wild Horse had been hunting since he was old enough to run. His father had taught him that the animals he hunted would kill him if he didn't kill them, but he had been eager to learn more; to become as good a predator as any animal. He had watched and listened and smelt. From the uneven sound of its breathing, Wild Horse sensed the young mammoth was nervous. He tried to breathe deeply and slowly, to fill the air around them with calmness. Spreading his arms wide to show he had no more spears, that he was no longer a threat, he looked deep into the creature's eyes.

He spoke softly. 'We have both shown courage this day. Let us both live that we might meet another time.'

They stayed motionless for what seemed an age. Wild Horse waited for the mammoth's first move, his body ready to spring in the opposite direction. He wasn't *afraid* to die, but he wasn't *ready* to die either. He flinched as an image of his brother's body, ravaged by a bear, flashed in his mind. Running Bear had been killed during the last Snow Moons but his passing was still raw.

Suddenly the mammoth raised its head and bellowed, sending the birds in the nearby trees screeching into the air. Then it stepped back, splitting Wild Horse's spear under its hoof before swerving away from him.

Wild Horse watched the beast lumber towards the rugged Land of Hills and felt his whole body sag with relief. He had survived to tell his father about his courage.

'What do you mean, you let the animal go?' Bear Face roared. 'You should have run after it.'

'But, Father, it had broken my spear.' Wild Horse held up the point he'd rescued from the splintered shaft. 'I'm lucky to be alive. I thought you'd be proud that I'd challenged the mammoth alone – like a brave hunter.'

He looked around, hoping for nods of support from the tribespeople who had looked up from their tasks, but they quickly returned to the sharpening of tools and scraping of hides. They knew better than to come between their chief and his son. His mother gazed up at the sky, as if she was thanking the Spirits for sparing Wild Horse's life, before moving away towards her shelter.

'Why did you only have one spear?' Bear Face bared his teeth. 'And why were you on your own, again? Running Bear would have had at least three spears – and as many hunters.'

Once more Wild Horse was compared to his dead brother. And worse, it was true: Running Bear always carried several spears. And he took other hunters with him, apart from that one time – his last hunt. Wild Horse felt as empty as a dry riverbed, unworthy of respect.

'As it let me live,' he stuttered, 'it deserved to live too.'

'Deserved to live!' bellowed the chief. 'You think an animal deserved to live? As my eldest son, the son of the great hunter Bear Face, you must bring food and honour to your tribe. A mammoth kill would have given us both. It is so long since we have eaten mammoth.' He licked his lips as if savouring the lost meat. 'But now you have shamed me and yourself.'

Wild Horse felt glances firing into him like spear-points, and he could hear his cousin Zuni sniggering. His two younger brothers, Grey Horse and Little Bear, looked down at the ground, as if sharing his humiliation.

As he stood alone, the honour Wild Horse had hoped for faded into the scrubland along with the mammoth he had failed to take.

'Chief Mogoll arrives in two days,' said Bear Face. 'A mammoth kill would have impressed him. I have had word that he has already visited other tribes during the Snow Moons to find a husband for his daughter. But who would want a boy who lets a mammoth escape?'

'I'm not ready for a wife, Father.' Wild Horse shuddered. 'I've only seen thirteen winters.'

'I'll decide when you're ready,' Bear Face said. 'A wife is exactly what you need. It will bring honour to our tribe.' He grabbed Wild Horse by the shoulders. 'It is time you stopped running off on your own. When Mogoll arrives, you will lead the hunters and bring back a mammoth for our feast.'

Zuni was suddenly there. His hair was pulled tightly off his face in a taut braid, emphasising his dark, darting eyes. Although three winters older than Wild Horse, he was not much taller. He stabbed his spear at the ground.

'*I* have led the hunters since Running Bear died,' he said. 'I should be the one who does it for Mogoll.'

'Brother,' said Zuni's father Great Wolf to his chief, 'it is Zuni's place to lead the hunters. He has done it well until now.'

'Yes,' said Bear Face, 'but now Wild Horse must take his brother's place. He is the eldest son of the chief and that is the way of this tribe.'

Zuni gave Wild Horse a look of pure hatred, then marched to his shelter, followed by Great Wolf.

Wild Horse cursed his dead brother. If Running Bear had still been alive he'd be the lead hunter. Although Wild Horse had always wanted to hunt as well as his brother, to run as fast as his brother, he didn't want to lead the hunters or the tribe.

But he could never admit that to his father.

Bear Face's greying hair hung loose over his hunched and weak shoulders, as if even his shoulders understood that a new leader would soon be needed. And Bear Face had now chosen his son's path; the only way Wild Horse could gain his father's respect was to hunt and kill animals, and also to somehow win Mogoll's daughter.

If only there was another way he could impress Mogoll. He didn't want to be married; he wanted to be free to hunt on his own, free to learn more about the animals they had to hunt for food.

'You'll need a new spear-shaft,' said Bear Face. 'Make sure it's strong and worthy enough for a lead hunter.' The old man glowered at his son, daring him to argue.

Wild Horse walked to the wood store at the edge of the camp, where they had settled for the winter Snow Moons. Their six shelters huddled between rocks. On the other side of the river, coarse grass savannah was scattered with trees. Beyond that lay many rivers and sinkholes, rocks, cliffs and caves.

The tribe had gathered and dried logs and branches. Some had been used to support the hide shelters. The thick logs had been stored for fires, but they had treated the branches with fatty oils scraped from under the skins of carcasses, for use as spear-shafts. Wild Horse chose the longest and strongest branch. Using tools made of chert and bone he crafted a spear to replace the one broken by the mammoth. And two more. He would never again walk with fewer than three spears.

As he worked, Wild Horse watched Zuni talking to Great Wolf by their shelter, saw how they cast angry glares at him. Wild Horse knew Zuni would not give up the role of lead hunter easily, and he wondered what his cousin and uncle were planning.

CHAPTER TWO

BLUE BIRD

Blue Bird clawed Burning Fire's face as she fought to save the tiny newborn, but the woman was bigger than Blue Bird and forced the creature under the surface of the shallow stream.

'Let Paska keep *one* of the puppies,' screamed Blue Bird, trying to scoop up the five lifeless bodies already lying in the water. 'Release it or I'll tell Paska to attack you!'

'You will not.' Her father Mogoll strode towards them from the camp.

Paska whimpered as she pawed at the bodies. Blue Bird knelt in the stream next to her and rubbed her face against her dog's fur.

'Burning Fire killed all the puppies,' she sobbed.

'And look what the wild she-cat of a daughter of yours has done to me.' The woman turned her bloodied cheek towards Mogoll. 'I shouldn't have to suffer so from a child.'

'I am not a child,' said Blue Bird. 'And I am the one who suffers, you snake!'

'Only a child would cry at such a thing,' said Burning Fire. 'I've done the right thing by getting rid of them.'

'It is the right thing, Blue Bird. We do not need puppies,' Mogoll said. 'We are getting ready to leave camp. You have no right to fight with Burning Fire. She is heavy with child. You must say sorry.'

Blue Bird knew that her father wouldn't take her side; he never did – not since that woman had given him two sons. But she would not show any regret for scratching Burning Fire's face. She gathered the six tiny bodies into the rough wooden bowl in which Burning Fire had carried them, and ran upstream, Paska close behind.

Nobody followed her. Nobody heard her crying, or saw her heaving shoulders as she laid the dead puppies on a flat rock. Four of them were grey with black splodges like Paska, but two were the colour of a muddy river.

Blue Bird wanted the Spirits to find their souls before the wolves or the vultures came to eat the remains. While she waited, she made a decision. She could not stay here. She had never known her own mother who had died giving birth to her, and now her father had another wife she didn't feel she belonged any more. She was going to run away.

She waited for darkness to fall before creeping back to the camp, expecting the tribe to be asleep. A hand grabbed her shoulder as she reached her shelter, and she jumped.

It was Burning Fire. Paska snarled.

'Let go of me or Paska will bite.'

The woman leant so close that her face almost touched Blue Bird's, the deep scratches visible even in the darkness, her breath reeking of raw meat.

'I'll make sure your father has that dog butchered,' she hissed. 'At sunrise, before we leave this camp, I'll tell Mogoll it will slow us down, that it is best to end its pathetic life before we set off.' Then she slapped Blue Bird so hard she fell to her knees.

Paska nuzzled Blue Bird as Burning Fire strode away. Hatred for her father's wife welled up inside her, and she shivered at the thought of losing Paska as well as the puppies. Now there could be no change of mind – she had to leave. And she had to be gone before sunrise.

Before that woman ordered Paska's death.

She crawled into the shelter she shared with her aunt Sacred Cloud and her daughter Fawn. They were asleep. Blue Bird quickly rolled all her belongings into her sleeping-fur: stone scrapers and fire-stones; sinew, a bone awl and needles; slabs of pemmican, nuts and dried berries; and a frayed rabbit-skin pouch with a wooden pot of Sacred Cloud's healing balm inside. She slung a water-skin across her shoulder, and checked that the hunting pouch tied to her belt held her knife and two spare points.

It was time to go.

She crawled out of the shelter. Blue Bird knew that Sacred Cloud and Fawn would look after each other, and hoped that they'd forgive her for leaving them. Looking up to the sky she asked the Spirits to bless her with a safe journey.

Sacred Cloud had told her many times about the place where she and Blue Bird's mother had grown up. She would go there and look for her mother's tribe. That was where she belonged. But first, she had to get away from this one.

She set off, walking beside the stream. The rippling sounds and the way it reflected the light from the moon and stars made it the easiest course to follow, but the howls of a wolf made her reach for Paska. Her hand trembled as she stroked the dog's neck. Paska wasn't a large dog – she stood not much higher than Blue Bird's knees – but it was easier being brave with Paska by her side. She gave Blue Bird the strength not to turn round, even when a whoosh of wings swept low over her head: an owl, clutching a mouse in its claws. She flinched but kept walking.

All night.

To think about the threats lurking in the darkness might send her back to what she so longed to leave behind.

When the stream disappeared underground Blue Bird followed the outskirts of dense woodland, which led over a ridge and down towards a river. As they drank, Blue Bird looked across the water to where a massive craggy rock jutted out of the darkness: it might be a good place to find shelter. Paska hadn't fallen behind once, though she must be exhausted after giving birth, and now the dog lay down panting – Blue Bird feared she might be too weak even to cross the river.

'Come on.' She squatted to pick up Paska, grasping the dog under her chest and rear legs, then waded across the river, using the remains of her own strength, grateful for the moonlight on the water to guide her across. 'We must find somewhere to rest,' she said, placing Paska on the ground.

They scrambled up the rock face. A dark hollow emerged as Blue Bird pulled herself up to a ledge. Half hidden by scrubby bushes was a cave like an open mouth. She only had to stoop a little to enter it, brushing away the spiders' webs that clung to her. It was dry and empty; a good place to shelter. Beetles scuttled away as she wrapped her sleeping-fur around her and snuggled next to Paska for warmth.

She didn't remember falling asleep, but the sound of voices woke her.

Voices she knew.

She moved to the entrance of the cave, clutching her spear, then dropped to the ground behind a bush and held her breath.

Her father and his hunters were looking at what must be her tracks on the other side of the river. The rest of the tribe waited behind them. She was sure they could all hear the pounding of her blood, deep inside her.

Finally Mogoll led the tribe downriver and Blue Bird breathed a sigh of relief. She watched Sacred Cloud hesitate, and wanted to call out, to reassure her aunt that she was still alive. Then Fawn took her mother's hand, and Blue Bird knew it was right she travelled alone. Neither had her strength and resilience. She would not have made it this far through the night if they'd been with her.

Burning Fire shouted that if Blue Bird had survived the night, she'd soon come crawling back to them because the dog would be dead.

Mogoll roared at Sacred Cloud not to linger.

Their harshness strengthened Blue Bird's resolve. She could not return. She *would* not return.

CHAPTER THREE

WILD HORSE

Wild Horse heard gasps around him as Mogoll's tribe approached their small camp. Most tribes had fewer than twenty people; Mogoll's numbered twice that. The chief wore the fur from several raccoon pelts, the ringed tail of one hanging from a wide belt of bison hide, and although he had seen as many winters as Bear Face, his shoulders were drawn back and his head held high, like a mountain lion.

So this was the chief that Wild Horse had to impress. He stifled a nervous shudder. *I must be strong*, he thought, pulling back his shoulders and raising his chin. He carried his presentation spear, decorated with the tail of a wolf. It had been his father's gift when he'd made his first lone kill.

The memory gave Wild Horse strength.

He was only six winters old and he'd followed his father's hunting party. Stumbling through the undergrowth, he'd come face to face with the wolf cub, separated from its kin by the hunters. The cub bared its teeth, snarling as it prepared to attack. Wild Horse's fear had flown with his spear, which he thrust into the animal's chest as it leapt towards him. When his father had hoisted Wild Horse on to one shoulder and the dead animal over the other, he'd called out that his son was a brave and true hunter. At that moment Wild Horse had felt his father's pride coursing through his whole body . . .

Wild Horse wanted his father to feel like that again. But the only way was to win Mogoll's daughter as his wife, a wife he didn't want. He'd rather face the mammoth again.

Mogoll strode towards Bear Face and stopped in front of him. 'I am Mogoll, chief of this tribe.'

Two young boys flanked the chief. Behind them stood a girl with a dark brow and eyes, slightly older than Wild Horse, and a woman heavy with child. Wild Horse noticed deep scratches scored the woman's cheek. A younger girl held the hand of another woman who was gazing at the sky, murmuring. The rest of the tribe stood further back.

Bear Face said, 'I am the chief of this tribe. They call me Bear Face. We greet you. We have meat ready for you.' His father seemed suddenly smaller as he stood before the visiting chief.

Mogoll raised his hand. 'Your greeting is accepted. I will eat with you, but I first need your hunters, to help search for my daughter.'

Wild Horse's spirits lifted. A lost daughter? Was it the one he was meant to win? He hoped so.

'Is she lost?' asked Bear Face.

'Blue Bird, my second daughter,' Mogoll replied. 'She disappeared in the night. We found tracks, but when they reached the river we could not see which way they led. I fear she may be drowned, or taken by wolves.'

'Don't say such things, Mogoll. I know she must be alive. The Spirits tell me,' said the woman who had been gazing up to the sky. Her voice fluttered like the wings of a fledgling.

'Sacred Cloud, it is not your place to speak.' Mogoll spoke with ice in his voice. 'I have listened to your concern and agreed to send back a search party. Now be quiet.'

Wild Horse glanced at the woman with the scratched face. She was whispering to the dark-eyed girl, who grinned and shrugged her shoulders.

'Your hunters know this area,' Mogoll said to Bear Face. 'If they set off now they might find her.'

Wild Horse's father turned to him, his expression fierce, and Wild Horse took a deep breath and stepped forward. 'As the son of Bear Face, I vow to find your daughter Blue Bird.'

Bear Face thrust his chest forward like a bull bison. 'My son Wild Horse is a good tracker. He will do as he says.'

'And I am Zuni, son of Great Wolf.' Zuni pushed past Wild Horse, making him stumble. 'I am the *best* tracker and I will find your daughter.'

Bear Face grimaced as Great Wolf gripped his son's shoulder, a broad smile spreading across his face.

Mogoll thumped his spear against the ground. 'This is better. Whoever finds Blue Bird, my lost daughter, will win my eldest daughter – Night Rain.' He turned to the dark-eyed girl behind him. 'Night Rain, see how lucky you are to have two fine hunters vying for you.'

She glared at Zuni and Wild Horse, her heavy brow as forbidding as her father's.

'Come, Mogoll,' said Bear Face, 'we can sit by the fire while the hunters begin their search.'

Zuni sidled close to Wild Horse. 'I will claim the prize of Mogoll's daughter.'

'You are welcome to her,' said Wild Horse, 'but you won't win. I have learnt more from the animals than you ever will.'

'I will not be insulted by some fool who spends more time looking at animals than killing them,' Zuni snarled. 'The Spirits have blessed me at last. I have waited for my chance since Running Bear died.'

'You never mourned him as you should,' said Wild Horse. 'He taught you everything he knew about hunting, was always by your side, yet you weren't there for him when he was killed.'

'He was careless, took chances. Now I take mine.'

'Running Bear was fearless, but not careless.'

'We all make mistakes. Yours is that you think you'll win this challenge.' Zuni leant even closer to Wild Horse. 'You're wrong. The girl is mine to win. With such a wife – the daughter of a mighty chief – I shall be ready to take over as chief of this tribe when it is Bear Face's time to meet the Spirits. It is my right.'

'Why should it be your right?'

'I was named for the river where the father of our fathers was born, and I feel that river in my blood. You could never lead a tribe, cousin. You are too wild, like the horse you are named for. Be warned – I am ready for a fight. And I'm going to win, whatever it takes.'

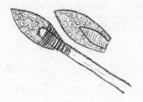

CHAPTER FOUR

WILD HORSE

Wild Horse and Zuni were to lead separate search parties. Wild Horse asked for Tall Tree, who had been a close friend of Running Bear, and Zuni took his younger brother, Dark Wolf.

They followed four of Mogoll's men back to the tracks they'd found by the edge of the woodland.

'It looks like she walked towards the river,' said Zuni at last, 'maybe to fill her water-skin, then headed towards the woodland. She would feel safer hiding amongst the trees rather than risk crossing the river. The rock on the other side is too high and the face steep for a girl to climb.'

Sharp-eyed as an owl, Wild Horse noticed a newly

broken branch on a tree clinging to the rock. He thought the opposite: the girl had crossed the river and scrambled up the rock face. There were scattered bushes to provide cover. He thought for a moment.

'It looks like you've worked out where she's gone,' he said, sighing heavily. 'Perhaps we should stay together and not split into two groups until we are inside the woodland.'

'No,' said Zuni. 'Leave the woodland to us. You cross the river, just in case that's where she went.'

'You know she won't be over there,' replied Wild Horse. 'You go into the woods then and we will follow the riverbank on this side, where it borders the trees. She might have stayed near the edge for light and water.'

Zuni looked annoyed and Wild Horse turned away to hide his smile. He'd out-foxed his cousin and distracted him from thinking about the other side of the river.

He watched Zuni and Dark Wolf walk into the woodland with two of Mogoll's hunters.

Thoughts buzzed around Wild Horse's mind like bees on blossom. Winning this test would bring him a wife, a wife he didn't want. Deliberately losing would mean he could stay free, but it would bring shame to his father. Again. And if Zuni won, he would forever taunt Wild Horse, and likely become chief. He could not live with that. There was no choice.

He had to beat his cousin.

'We can cover more ground if we split up.' Wild Horse said to Tall Tree, then turned to the other two hunters from Mogoll's tribe. 'It will be best if you go with Tall Tree, following this side of the riverbank. I'll cross the river and climb the rock face – there'll be a good view from the top. I might catch you up later. If I do not, meet me back here, as the sun starts its descent. If you don't find her, hopefully I will, and then we will beat that lump of bison dung, Zuni.'

Tall Tree frowned a little, showing Wild Horse he knew he was up to something, but he wasn't sure what. 'The Spirits go with you, Wild Horse,' he said at last. 'It will be good to beat Zuni.'

Wild Horse expected one of Mogoll's men to ask why they didn't split into pairs. But being the chief's son did have its merits after all; they followed his commands without question.

He pulled off his moccasins and leggings before wading across the river. It reminded him of when he had crossed the stream to face the mammoth, with no time to remove anything. So much had happened since then. The cold water lapped around his legs, nipping at his flesh, as if telling him to think of what lay ahead, not of what lay before.

As Wild Horse clambered up the rock he was sure the girl had come this way – there were small signals that many wouldn't see: a few fallen stones; a branch bent as if grasped at. The droppings of a dog confirmed his instinct.

Not that he expected to find her. If he escaped from his tribe he'd get as far away as possible, so he expected the girl to be long gone, though he feared he might find her injured, or worse, discover her remains mauled by a wolf or some creature of the night. He paused on a narrow ledge to watch Tall Tree dashing along the opposite riverbank, the other two tribesmen at his heels. They poked their spears at undergrowth, looking for traces of the missing girl. They wouldn't find anything.

Wild Horse knew that he could trust Tall Tree, who never went anywhere without at least four spears; knew that he would make his way along the river as he'd been told to, even though he was probably wondering what Wild Horse was up to. Tall Tree was four winters older than him, and he had shared Wild Horse's grief when Running Bear had died. He'd never been able to under-stand why his friend had been out hunting alone on the day he had been killed by a bear.

'I have no proof,' Tall Tree had said to Wild Horse as they sat around the campfire that night, 'but I find it strange that Zuni came running back to the camp, without even a scratch, shouting that he'd found Running Bear dead, as if by accident. I do not say he caused your brother's death, but I think he goaded him into taking some risk. They often dared each other. I wish they had not left me behind. I could have stopped them . . .'

As Wild Horse watched Tall Tree disappear out of view, with thoughts of Running Bear crowding his mind, a boulder the size of his head hurtled down and landed at his feet.

'Drop your spears or you'll have mine right between your eyes.' The voice came from above, the voice of a girl.

Wild Horse looked up, but the sun was shining directly

into his eyes. He blinked, cursing. *She's chosen her position too well.*

'I can see where you are,' he bluffed, 'and I don't think I need worry as you're clearly a bad shot or you'd have hit me with the rock.'

Another boulder plunged down, this time knocking the raised spear out of his hand.

'I told you to drop your spears. Maybe now you'll realise that if I'd wanted to hit you with the first boulder then I would have aimed at your head, not your foot. I have no desire to kill you. I just want you to leave me alone.'

'I am Wild Horse, son of Bear Face, and I'm looking for Blue Bird, daughter of Mogoll, who is lost.'

'I am Blue Bird and I'm not *lost*. I ran away. Just go, and leave me alone.'

Wild Horse put down his spears and held up his arms, partly to shield his eyes and partly to show that he posed no threat. He moved slowly into shade to avoid the dazzle of the sun, and looked up.

The girl was smaller than he was, her slender frame outlined by the sun giving her a spirit-like appearance. Her black hair hung in two long braids over her shoulders, and she wore a wrap skirt of deerskin over leggings which were attached to her moccasins with hide ties. Her shoulders looked broad under the rabbit-skin top, and she knew how to hold a spear; her arm was bent ready to unleash it. A hunting pouch tied to her belt hung heavily – maybe with a knife and spare points, like his own. Beside her a grizzled grey dog crouched, teeth bared.

Her face was taut with determination as she stared straight at him. She looked like a hunter – not like a girl who would be easy to capture.

CHAPTER FIVE

BLUE BIRD

Blue Bird studied the young hunter on the ledge below her. His hair was tied in a loose braid falling down the back of his short tunic of bison hide. A deerskin breechcloth, tucked over the belt from which his hunting pouch hung, revealed long muscular legs. He returned her stare with eyes the colour of burnt wood.

Even though Paska had nuzzled her awake at the sound of voices, she hadn't had time to escape, which is why she had thrown the first boulder – it had seemed too risky to unleash her only spear. But the boy wasn't moving. She raised her voice.

'I said go away, Wild Horse, son of Bear Face.'

'Why have you run away?'

'That's nothing to do with you.'

'Your father is worried.'

'I don't think so.'

'Then why did he send out search parties?'

'I don't know,' said Blue Bird. 'I'm sure he's glad to be rid of me.'

'Why do you say that?'

'I'm not the son he wanted. Any use I was to him was spoilt by the arrival of my brothers.'

'What about your mother? The woman with child?'

'That is not my mother. My mother died when I was born. That vicious vixen is Burning Fire, my father's wife.' Wild Horse knelt down. 'I said, go away.'

'I would, but the trouble is that if I don't find you then it's likely that Zuni will. And when he does you'll wish that you'd have let me be your rescuer.'

'But I've told you – I don't want a rescuer. And who is Zuni?'

Wild Horse shrugged. 'My cousin. At the moment he's looking in the woodland on the other side of the river, but when he doesn't find you there he'll look elsewhere, here maybe.'

'Well, I'll be gone by then.'

'Gone where?'

Blue Bird said nothing. She didn't want to admit she hadn't worked out where to go next.

'Even if you set off now, we'll be bound to catch up with you. If not today, then the next. If I don't bring you back,

Zuni will gloat that I failed to find you. It will boost his determination to win, and he will track you down like an animal.'

'What do you mean – win?'

Wild Horse sighed. 'We're rivals. The one who finds you gets to be the husband of your sister, Night Rain.'

'You are welcome to her – she is not a good sister. And she doesn't deserve rivals.'

'Your father Mogoll must think she does. And it is my father's will that I should win. But Zuni is ready for a fight; he is determined to beat me.'

'What about you?'

'What about me?' said Wild Horse.

'Are you determined to win? I warn you now that Night Rain does not have a sweet nature.'

'I am not ready for a wife, but I can't let Zuni beat me.'

'If you are not ready for a wife, why are you taking part in the challenge? Why don't you just leave me here?'

'I can't. Finding you will bring me respect from my tribe.'

'I've already said I don't want to be found – can't you understand that?' Blue Bird pleaded.

'If I fail to find you, then the shame of losing to my cousin will weigh too heavy on my shoulders. And my father will feel so dishonoured if I lose this challenge that he will cast me out of the tribe.'

'I feel your torment, son of Bear Face, but you should understand my misery too – such misery that I have cast myself out of my tribe. Is your fear of shame so cruel that you'd drag me back to a life I am desperate to leave behind?' Blue Bird shook her spear to show her despair.

'Come down here, daughter of Mogoll. You're asking me to give up the chance of gaining honour for myself and my tribe, so tell me why I should leave you here, why I should risk shame.'

'Why should I trust you?'

'I am alone – you watched me cross the river on my own. If you come down, you can keep hold of your spear and I'll leave mine on the ground.'

'Be ready, Paska,' Blue Bird called as she climbed down the rock, clutching her spear and nudging Wild Horse's spears out of reach with her foot. The dog growled, head down, ready to leap at Wild Horse if she gave the signal.

'I've never met a girl who liked throwing spears,' said Wild Horse. 'But why did you run away?'

Blue Bird looked at the boy; the bleakness in his eyes matched hers. And even if Paska could hold him off while she packed up her belongings, they wouldn't get far before he alerted the other hunters. She had to make him understand. Her eyes filled with tears.

'Burning Fire killed Paska's puppies. She hated me training her sons to hunt, and made them tell Mogoll they no longer needed the help of a girl. Then she drowned all Paska's puppies, to spite me. I managed to pull one out of the water – I think it was still alive – but she was too strong for me and plunged it back into the river. I pleaded with her. I screamed. I scratched her.'

'I saw marks on her face,' said Wild Horse. 'You must

fight like a sabretooth.'

'If I need to. I had to get away from her, especially when she said she would have Paska killed too. Though it meant leaving my dear aunt, who has been the only mother I've known.'

'Where will you go?'

'Many times Sacred Cloud has told me tales about her childhood with my mother – about the land where they travelled: the mountains and rivers; the birds and animals and fish they caught and ate; the plants they used for medicines. That is where I want to go, to find my mother's tribe.'

'Do you know where it is?'

'Not exactly,' said Blue Bird, not daring to admit she had never been there. 'Sacred Cloud said it was many moons away, beyond the Great Plains, the other side of a river known as the Great River. A river they hadn't crossed again in my lifetime, though they had passed along the sunset side of it since. She remembered looking back at the sun rising over her tribe's camp as she and my mother left their family behind. And as they travelled the sun passed overhead and they walked towards the setting sun. Sacred Cloud told me that when she dies she knows her spirit will fly to where the sun rises, to find her family before it soars up to the stars. That is where I shall look for my mother's family.'

'How will you find them on your own?'

'The sun and the Spirits in the stars will guide me.' Blue Bird stood up, glancing skywards, as Sacred Cloud did.

But as she turned back she glimpsed a group of hunters approaching in the distance on the opposite riverbank. Fear clutched her throat and she almost dropped her spear.

'It's my father!' she gasped.

Wild Horse jumped up.

'What are you going to do?' said Blue Bird, unable to move as the dread of returning to Mogoll and Burning Fire gripped her so tight she could barely breathe. Her voice was little more than a whisper. 'Please don't tell them you've found me.'

CHAPTER SIX

WILD HORSE

Wild Horse saw Blue Bird's whole body shudder. She looked desperate.

'Are you sure that you'd rather be out here on your own, than in a camp with the safety of your tribe?' he asked. 'Wolves and sabretooth cats hunt these parts, and only two sunrises ago I saw a mammoth on this side of the river. These are all dangers more fearsome than Burning Fire or your father.'

'I am sure. It is good to be free,' said Blue Bird, her eyes flashing. 'I won't go back, and Paska and I will fight if we have to.'

'It is a brave path you choose, Blue Bird. I honour

your courage.'

'What will you say?'

Wild Horse looked at the approaching hunters, Bear Face and Grey Wolf either side of Mogoll, each most likely telling the visiting chief how they expected their son to be the victor. Then he glanced at Blue Bird, standing proud and ready to fight for her freedom. How could he let her down?

'I'll tell Mogoll that he should be proud to have a daughter who is so good at hiding her tracks that we lost her trail,' he said finally.

A shimmer of relief lit up Blue Bird's face. 'Thank you, Wild Horse. May the Spirits of the stars always guide you.'

'That is kind, but it is you who needs their help. You are safe for now, but who knows what lies ahead? Beware the wolves. And Zuni. He is determined to find you, to beat me at this challenge and win your sister.'

Blue Bird leant forwards and traced the shape of a star on his forehead. 'I will remember your kindness always.'

Wild Horse watched the girl soar up the rock, her tread soft and light as a bird's. A bird with strong wings, strong enough to throw a spear. He put his hand to his forehead. Her touch had been as soft as her tread, yet he was sure he could feel the outline of the star, as if a force had fluttered through her fingertips, leaving an unseen mark so that he'd never forget her.

She disappeared behind bushes, Paska beside her. Just in time. He could see Tall Tree and the two hunters running from one direction along the riverbank as the chiefs and their hunters approached from the other.

He scrambled back down the rock face. 'May your Spirits be with you,' he whispered as he looked up to where he'd seen Blue Bird, trying to ignore the twist of anxiety tugging at him. How long could she survive on her own?

But first he had to make sure she wasn't found by Zuni. And then, somehow, he had to find another way of gaining honour with his father and Mogoll. He splashed across the river.

Zuni was waiting for him at the edge of the woods, with Dark Wolf and Mogoll's other two hunters.

'Look at me,' said Wild Horse, pretending to shiver as he pulled on his leggings and moccasins. 'I wasted my time getting cold and wet by crossing the river. You were right, Zuni. The girl must have gone into the woods. You have succeeded where I have failed. Where is she?'

Zuni's dark eyes narrowed. 'We searched thoroughly; there were no further tracks. Are you sure she didn't cross the river?'

'Do you think I'd come back empty-handed if I'd found anything?' said Wild Horse. 'I climbed high to see further. If you look carefully you can see the branch I broke. But you can wade across the cold water yourself if you want to check if I missed anything.'

Wild Horse knew Zuni wasn't interested in broken branches. His cousin was too busy seething about his failure to find Blue Bird.

He let Zuni stride past him to meet the advancing chiefs.

Mogoll spoke first. 'Do you come to tell me that you have found my daughter?'

'We did not find any further clues along the river,' said Zuni, 'and we all agreed your daughter had gone into the woodland. I led my men through the trees. Wild Horse let Tall Tree take your hunters along the riverbank while he wasted his time splashing across the river. We saw animal tracks, droppings, but no signs of the girl.'

Wild Horse saw his father shake his head in dismay. For a moment he considered telling them he'd seen Blue Bird's tracks, but that they showed she was long gone. He soon cast such thoughts away. He must not betray her.

'Mogoll,' he said, pausing to gather his thoughts, 'it is possible that your daughter has been attacked and killed by one of the predators that roam these parts.'

'Yes, I fear that is what has happened,' said Mogoll, carelessly.

Wild Horse paused. Was the chief really so ready to accept his daughter's fate? 'But as we found no trace of such an attack,' he went on, 'is it possible that she has some hunting skills? And is able to hide tracks as well as find them?'

Bear Face shook his head, his brow bleak as a storm-filled sky. 'Girls don't hunt.'

'But the boy is right.' Mogoll stepped forward and laid his hand on Wild Horse's shoulder. 'For too long I was not blessed with a son, so Blue Bird joined me on many hunts.'

'Then she must surely be a daughter to be proud of.' Wild Horse watched Bear Face's face lighten as he realised his son's remarks had impressed the other chief. So he had gained favour with Mogoll, and given his father pleasure.

Best of all, he could see the storm raging behind Zuni's eyes.

But he needed to stop them crossing the river to the rock face. He didn't know how long she intended to stay there. If her plan was to follow a course to where the sun rises, she would walk downriver. But that led back towards the camp. Hopefully she'd know that and instead head across the Land of Hills. A longer route, but a safer one, where many hills of rock, like the one where Blue Bird had found shelter, jutted out of the ground.

Wild Horse wanted to give Blue Bird time to get away.

'If she still lives she might have taken cover somewhere,' he added, 'knowing you'd pick up her tracks and then lose them by the river.'

'The boy thinks well,' said Mogoll, 'but he thinks like a man, like a hunter. Not like a girl.'

'But you taught your daughter well,' – Wild Horse could see Mogoll was pleased by the flattery – 'so she might think like a hunter too. There is a bison trail nearby that passes the Sacred Rock. It would be an easy route for her to pick up.'

'The Sacred Rock,' said Mogoll. 'It is known for its spiritual powers. It is many winters since I saw it. I had not realised we were so close.'

'If we set off now we can get back to the camp as darkness starts to fall.'

'Then we must go. I will touch it to ask the Spirits for

another son.'

And to find your daughter, thought Wild Horse, though he was glad to be leading the chief away from her.

'And if we meet a herd of bison my son can show you how well he hunts,' said Bear Face.

'A hunt as well?' said Mogoll. 'Even better.'

Wild Horse turned away from the chiefs to hide his smile. He'd outwitted them all, gained praise from both Mogoll and his father, and given Blue Bird the chance to flee.

Tall Tree caught the edge of the smile, though, and gave him a careful look. Wild Horse ignored it. He was enjoying the sight of Zuni stomping towards Great Wolf, his teeth bared like a raging sabretooth.

CHAPTER SEVEN

BLUE BIRD

Hidden by the entrance to her cave, Blue Bird held her breath as she watched Wild Horse talk first to the hunter who must be Zuni, and then to her father. They were surrounded by other hunters. She wanted to believe Wild Horse wouldn't tell them where she was.

But there was much talking. Too much talking. Blue Bird trembled as she gripped her spear so tightly it hurt her hand.

Then Wild Horse led the hunters up the ridge, away from the river. He looked over his shoulder when they reached the top of it. Did he know she was watching him?

She did not loosen the grip on her spear until they disappeared from her sight. Blinking back tears, she heaved a huge sigh of relief. At last, free and on her own. Apart from Paska, of course. Dear Paska, still recovering from giving birth to six puppies, with none left alive.

She wanted to continue her journey, but the dog needed to rest; she was still weak from walking through the night. And only now did Blue Bird realise how hungry she was. She had packed some dried food, but the journey ahead of her would take many moons to complete. She needed to save as much as possible, and build up supplies, so she should try and catch something. For Paska, as well as for herself.

Now that the hunters had gone, birdsong and the sounds of the rushing river filled her ears as she scanned the trees on the other side of the river. The woodland had wildlife and places to hide, but it would be easy to get lost in there. This rock offered more protection, and the ground below was littered with enough bushes and trees to provide firewood. Hopefully she'd find something to hunt on this side of the river. She would stay for another sunset, while she worked out a plan. She'd never had a plan before, had been free-spirited until that sly snake Burning Fire had stifled her.

She had to trust that Wild Horse would not tell anybody that he'd seen her. If he was going to tell her father, surely he'd have done it there and then. But he hadn't, and Blue Bird had to place her faith in him, even though they'd only just met.

He'd probably expect her to move on, so by staying where she was, she should be safe. She would have to build a fire in the cave, both to keep them warm as the night chill fell, and to help ward off predators. Wild Horse had warned her that sabretooth cats and wolves preyed in these parts. Creatures she'd have to face alone.

'But I've come this far, so I can go on,' she said to herself.

She held her spear up to the sky, asking the Spirits to send her easy prey. Her bravery began to ebb away, flowing downstream with the river. 'But I am not truly alone,' she muttered. 'The Spirits are with me.'

Blue Bird rolled out the bearskin she slept in. It contained everything she had brought with her. The frayed rabbit-skin pouch and balm were her most prized possessions – Blue Bird always carried some of Sacred Cloud's balm, for it had good healing powers, and soothed both cuts and hunting wounds. She wished she had also brought root from the plant used to make the balm, as chewing it could ease aching teeth and stomach pains, and lessen hunger.

She held the pouch against her chest. It had been sewn by her mother, soft rabbit skin with fine stitches of sinew. It was her only link with the mother she had never known. Stroking its softness gave her comfort and hope that she would find her mother's family.

But it also reminded Blue Bird of her first solo kill – a rabbit – and the thrill of taking it back to Mogoll. She closed her eyes as she pictured the look of pride on his face when he held up the rabbit to show off to the tribe. It was not usual for girls to go hunting, especially one as young as six winters.

'You have done well, daughter of mine,' he had said to Blue Bird. 'I was hoping that a son would give me this moment. I have not been blessed with one, but my daughter does so instead.'

But later she'd heard him say to one of the hunters, words that still scratched her ears: 'She did well enough for a daughter, but I feel sure a son would do better than a rabbit for his first kill.'

She grabbed her spear. A rabbit would fill her belly now.

'Time to go hunting,' she said to Paska, and the dog followed her as she clambered down to the river.

As she walked along the bank, she gazed back up at the huge craggy rock, which jutted upwards like it was trying to escape from the ground that grasped it. There were other ledges above her cave which might hide more caves. Below the rock, the scrubland was scattered with trees and large boulders. Animals might gather to drink by the boulders which bordered the riverbank. Just before sunset would be a good time to catch them, she knew. She started looking out for droppings, hoof marks or paw prints, as well as signs of anything else to eat – maybe fish or frogs, though with the Snow Moons still skulking perhaps it was a little early for frogs.

She saw nothing.

For a moment she imagined Wild Horse running towards her, those long legs galloping like the horse he was named for. As she shook off the image she recalled how much she'd told him; more than she'd meant to. There was something about him – something she had liked. A gentleness?

'Poor Wild Horse,' she muttered. 'You seem too good a person to end up with my spiteful sister.'

Paska's bark jolted her in time to see a snake slithering away into some bushes. Blue Bird jabbed her spear into the foliage, but the meal was gone. She nearly cursed Paska for frightening away the snake, but it was her own fault. The dog was trained to keep still and silent when Blue Bird was hunting, and only barked to warn of danger that Blue Bird hadn't noticed. The snake might have been venomous.

'Good dog.' She patted Paska. 'I must stay alert. The snakes must be coming out of their winter sleep.'

She moved swiftly but stealthily, Paska at her heels, her spear at the ready. If only she had another spear-shaft, she thought. Then, if she just injured an animal with her first throw, a second spear would finish the kill. At least she had a knife, spare points and fore-shafts.

It might be better to hunt on the other side of the river? She reached the place where the river widened and was shallower, with large flat rocks she could use as stepping stones. But she didn't get across. This time she saw the snake first. And there was a loose boulder next to her.

With one movement she scooped up the boulder and flipped it towards the snake. The snake whipped its tail round to slide away, but Blue Bird's boulder landed on its head.

Perfect. Blue Bird grabbed her knife and cut away the snake's body, leaving the smashed head under the boulder. She held it in front of her. Not very big, it stretched from her waist to the ground, but would satisfy their hunger for the rest of the day at least.

'We have food, Paska. Thank you, Spirits,' she called up to the sky.

She hurried back to the cave, collecting wood on the way. Then she rubbed her fire-stones together until her arms ached – but at last a spark ignited a dry twig, and she held her hands round it until the flame grew bright, gradually adding bigger twigs to build up a fire. She set two rocks into the fire, and as they grew hot she laid the snake over them. The skin crackled and sputtered, and the flames spat. Paska lay on the ground, her head close to the fire, her nose twitching.

Blue Bird waited as long as her stomach would allow before lifting the snake away from the hot rocks. She burnt her fingers and dropped it, so pierced it with a spear-point and laid it across a flat boulder at the edge of the cave. The sharp edge of her stone knife sliced through the crisped skin. She threw the first piece to Paska, who gulped it down, then sliced another chunk for herself. Sitting cross-legged in front of the fire, she ate rapidly, then slowed to savour each mouthful. Snake had never tasted so good.

CHAPTER EIGHT

WILD HORSE

The vast pink dome of the Sacred Rock could be seen at a distance from any direction. It imposed itself on the rolling landscape with such force it was no wonder that tribes considered it a sacred place. Trees, shrubs and cacti grew thickly round its base, thinning out at the upper reaches where lichen and mosses grew, and it bound together caves and springs and ledges. *So many places to hide*, thought Wild Horse as he walked round it. *If Blue Bird had come here she'd never have been found.*

Mogoll knelt. 'I will lay hands on the Rock so that I might ask for my unborn child to be a son. A third son would be a blessing from the Spirits of the Rock.'

Blue Bird seemed forgotten. Leaving Mogoll to speak to the Spirits, with Zuni and the others staying close to the chief, Wild Horse climbed halfway up the Sacred Rock and scanned the horizon. Dust was rising in the distance, along the shallow valley which curved around the rising sun side of the Rock.

Bison.

'A herd!' he called out as he scrambled back to the hunters. 'Bison heading our way!'

'Hush,' said Bear Face. 'Mogoll is not finished.'

Zuni snorted, and Wild Horse halted, realising what he'd interrupted.

Mogoll stopped chanting. 'How many?' he said.

'It is a big herd.'

'Well done. Show me.'

Bear Face's frown eased into a smile as Zuni's smirk soured into a scowl. Mogoll said, 'As the two challengers failed to find Blue Bird, it is time for a new contest. Wild Horse will lead half the men on one flank, and Zuni the other. The better hunter shall be the husband of Night Rain.'

'Wild Horse knows how to direct the bison towards a cliff in the direction of our camp,' Bear Face boasted. 'He can stampede the herd over it. There will be many kills.'

Wild Horse shook his head. *A waste of meat – many carcasses would end up rotting.* It was Running Bear who had enjoyed stampeding bison. And it was wrong to split the hunters into two bands – they should work together to hunt such a large herd. But Wild Horse couldn't question what had been said by the two chiefs; he would have to follow Mogoll's directions.

As they moved towards the herd, along the treeline that bordered the valley, Zuni and his hunters crossed to the other side. So far the herd hadn't detected them. Wild Horse knew they had to make sure the beasts weren't alerted until they passed the Sacred Rock and neared the cliff. Bison were known for their ability to discern danger, for their great senses of smell and hearing.

Hiding behind bushes, Wild Horse and his men waited for the herd to pass – so many beasts that they filled the width of the valley. It was the biggest herd Wild Horse had ever seen. The air was filled with snorts and grunts and the thud of hooves and the stench of stale animal sweat. As the rear of the herd drew closer to the hunters, Wild Horse remained alert for any signals of fear the animals might send: raised heads or twitching ears. He couldn't see Zuni's men on the other side of the herd, had to trust his cousin was also vigilant.

He glanced at the three elders standing on a low ledge on the Sacred Rock – Bear Face and Grey Wolf either side of Mogoll, each hoping his son would be the victor. He would have to complete this task so that Bear Face could stand proud. Again he cursed his older brother for dying.

The bison sometimes paused to protect their young. It reminded Wild Horse of a time when he'd seen a pack of wolves following a herd of bison. He was meant to be hunting, but he'd sensed he would learn more by watching.

The herd had felt the threat and grouped together, surrounding their calves as they ran. One calf had tripped, fallen behind, and been brought down by the lead wolf. The calf's mother and four other bison had turned round. They had seen off the wolves, allowing the calf to get up and run back to the herd with its rescuers. The wolves didn't give up; they knew they'd injured the calf so trailed behind the herd, hoping for another chance.

The wolves had worked together. The bison had worked together. Wild Horse and Zuni were working *against* each other. At least he had Tall Tree with him. He made hand signals to the band of hunters close behind him, still careful to avoid disturbing the herd, waiting for the right time. He had to believe that Zuni and his men would be patient too. They still weren't close enough to the cliff.

When the herd stopped to graze Wild Horse fell to his belly and so did his men.

Then sharp shouts ricocheted through the stillness from the other side of the herd. Zuni.

The animals' heads jerked up, and dust flew in the air as they bolted.

'Dung breath,' yelled Wild Horse as he and his men leapt to their feet. 'What does that brainless son of a skunk think he's doing?'

Zuni must have set them going. Too soon. And if the herd scattered they'd be lucky to make one kill, never mind charge some to their deaths.

Sure enough the herd broke up, and the rear group

turned towards Wild Horse and his hunters: forty or fifty bulks of bison charging at them, their hooves hammering the ground.

Thud, thud, thud.

Kicking up dust, snorting and stamping.

Thud, thud, thud.

It was happening so fast, yet to Wild Horse every beat of a hoof seemed slow and lingering. Was this how you felt when you were about to die? Was this Zuni's plan? To startle the herd so they might strike down Wild Horse and his hunters? No doubt Zuni would pretend sadness afterwards, and blame Wild Horse for causing it.

It's not going to happen, cousin, he thought. *It is not my time to die.* He shouted at his men, who were turning to run away, 'We can't outrun them. We'll be trodden to death. You must stamp your feet. Holler.'

'He is right,' said Tall Tree, running to Wild Horse's side, shouting and waving his arms.

One of Mogoll's men yelled above the thunder of the herd, 'What does he know? He's just a boy.'

'He understands animals,' shouted Tall Tree. 'Together we can frighten them into turning away. Running alone, we'll all be trampled.'

Wild Horse could wait no longer. He'd rather die running towards the bison than running away from them. He sprinted towards them, shrieking, sensed that at last Mogoll's men were following. He threw his first spear into the ground in front of the charging beasts, to startle them, and the other hunters did the same. The front bison slowed and hesitated, churning up choking dust.

This was their chance to make a kill. As the bison turned, one of the beasts was slower than the rest, possibly injured; this would be the one that wolves would hunt. Wild Horse lunged forwards, took aim and hurled his second spear. It found its target, in the side of the neck. Wild Horse had his next spear ready, but before he threw it Tall Tree's flew past him. The other hunters did the same and the beast fell to the ground.

It was a good kill.

Wild Horse thanked the Great Spirit, but it was Tall Tree who deserved most thanks. And as the noise and the dust from the stampede settled, he realised something else: there was no sign of Zuni.

CHAPTER NINE

WILD HORSE

Wild Horse sliced through the underbelly of the bison with his stone knife and yanked back the skin. Carefully he pulled out the entrails before they spoilt the meat. They would have to butcher as much of the animal as they could carry back to the camp, leaving the rest for the vultures and the wolves, or the sabretooth cats.

Tall Tree cut round the horns to remove them. 'These will please Mogoll and Bear Face.'

'They don't look pleased,' said Wild Horse as he watched the three elders approach.

'What happened to the stampede?' called out Bear Face.

'Zuni set them off too soon.' Wild Horse knew that nobody would believe him if he accused Zuni of deliberately panicking the herd in his direction.

Grey Wolf frowned. 'Zuni would have stood a better chance with your help. Why didn't you follow him?'

'The herd was breaking up and there weren't enough of us to control them,' said Wild Horse, and he gouged at the bison's head with his knife, imagining it to be Zuni's blood squirting out.

Wild Horse looked up at Bear Face, but his father's face was tight with disappointment. 'Just one kill, from a herd of that size?'

'See how much meat there is,' said Tall Tree, trying to help. 'We shall eat well.'

'Careful with that hide, boy.' Mogoll stood over Wild Horse.

Wild Horse squirmed under the chief's gaze. 'If we spend too long here, skinning and butchering, the big cats will pick up the scent and come for their share. They will attack us if they're hungry. We need to get back before nightfall.'

'Watch your tongue or you'll lose it.' Mogoll leant closer. 'If you want to please me, you will make a good job of that hide. Remove it quickly while the body is still warm and it should pull away easily.'

'Yes,' agreed Bear Face. 'Tall Tree, you help Wild Horse with the skinning while the others butcher the flesh. The hide can be properly scraped at the camp. There'll be plenty left for the big cats and vultures.'

It was Running Bear who used to skin hides with Tall Tree, not me, Wild Horse wanted to shout.

Great Wolf paced round them, then Wild Horse heard him call, 'Here comes Zuni. See what he brings us.'

Wild Horse looked up. Zuni and his men approached slowly. Swinging between four of them was a calf tied by its legs to a branch they were carrying.

'They travel so slow, you'd think they were carrying a mighty mammoth, not a baby bison,' said Wild Horse under his breath, and Tall Tree laughed.

'That looks like tender young meat,' said Mogoll.

'Not some dried-out carcass.' Great Wolf couldn't conceal his delight, adding, 'Zuni is a son to be proud of.'

Mogoll's face turned dark. 'But one of my men is injured. It is Falcon, my best hunter. That is why they walk so slowly.'

Wild Horse severed the last section of the hide from sinew and muscle. Raising his bloodied hands to his face, he spread his fingers and dragged red stripes across his cheeks – it was something Running Bear had always done after a good kill, a sign that his had been the first spear to pierce the animal. If Bear Face wanted him to act like his brother, Wild Horse thought, perhaps he should try and become his brother.

Tall Tree frowned. 'You don't have to do that. You are Wild Horse,' he said quietly, 'and you're already a better hunter than Running Bear.'

'My father doesn't think so.'

'He doesn't see what I see.' Tall Tree took one side of the

hide and prodded Wild Horse to hold the other as he stood up. 'Wild Horse has worked well, Chief Mogoll. See what a good hide it is.'

'There's a man missing,' shouted Mogoll, ignoring them.

Wild Horse let the hide drop to the ground. Tall Tree had spoken up for him, but it was useless. All chance of honour was gone.

'Falcon needs help,' called Zuni.

'What happened?' Mogoll rushed towards them, followed by Bear Face and Great Wolf. 'Where's Lightning?'

'My stupid cousin frightened the herd with his shouting and jumping,' Zuni snarled, looking at Wild Horse. 'We were circling round the far side of the herd when they turned towards us. Lightning stumbled and was trampled by many hooves. Falcon tried to save him – he is lucky to be alive, but Lightning did not live. We placed his body where the Spirits could find his soul.'

Accusing faces turned towards Wild Horse. He saw Dark Wolf open his mouth as if he was going to say something, but closed it when Zuni glowered at him. Falcon nodded at Zuni.

'You lie, cousin,' said Wild Horse. 'It was you who alarmed the bison. We were on our bellies when your hunters panicked the beasts and they came straight at us. We were forced to run at them and shout or we'd have all been dead.'

'It is you who lie, Wild Horse. You were so determined to win the challenge that you pushed the herd at us. That is why we have one man badly wounded and another dead, whereas yours all seem to be unharmed.'

'Wild Horse tells the truth,' said Tall Tree. 'The bison swerved towards us. We had to defend ourselves.'

Mogoll's hunters looked up from the butchering. They agreed the bison did turn towards them.

'We were going to run away,' said one, 'but Wild Horse said we'd die if we didn't holler and charge at the herd to turn them away from us. I don't know if we'd be alive now if we hadn't done that.'

'So you admit to shouting and driving the herd towards us,' said Zuni.

'We heard Wild Horse's call to his hunters,' said Falcon. 'He must have known where we were when they forced the herd in our direction. Lightning would still be alive if they hadn't acted so wildly, and I wouldn't be injured.'

Mogoll turned to Wild Horse. 'This should not have happened,' he roared. 'I have lost a good hunter.'

'Lightning was brave to the end,' said Zuni. 'An end which came too soon because Wild Horse, who says he understands animals, managed to panic them.'

Zuni's malevolence gouged into Wild Horse like a mastodon tusk.

'See what your wildness has caused,' growled Bear Face.

'Why don't you believe me?' asked Wild Horse. 'I couldn't see Zuni or his hunters. You wouldn't doubt my story if I was Running Bear.'

'If you were Running Bear none of this would have happened,' said Bear Face.

No, it wouldn't, thought Wild Horse. Tall Tree was wrong; he wasn't better than his brother. Running Bear had been a good leader as well as a good hunter. Although Wild Horse could hunt well, he was not born to lead. Running Bear used to playfully chase him away and tell him to track and hunt on his own. Maybe he had known that was better for his younger brother. Or maybe he had just thought Wild Horse was a pest and in the way.

Wild Horse trudged back to camp, the loss of Running Bear again heavy on his shoulders, along with the weight of the bison hide.

Darkness was descending as they reached the camp. Mogoll's tribe had set up their shelters on the edge of the woodland, behind the shelters of Wild Horse's people. Three or four saplings had been cut down for each shelter, bent towards each other and tied at the top with sinew and roots, forming a frame for the hides wrapped round them. The biggest shelter, which Wild Horse knew must be Mogoll's, used several pairs of saplings, linked by a branch ridge pole over which several hides were draped.

Two figures ran towards them: Blue Bird's aunt and her daughter.

'Where's Blue Bird? Did you find her?' Sacred Cloud's face was grazed with grief and fear.

'Never mind Blue Bird,' said Mogoll. 'Falcon is badly injured. You must see to his wounds. And we have a loss – Lightning is dead. When we praise the Spirits for the meat we bring we must ask them to greet a great hunter.'

'I am sorry for the loss of Lightning and will ask the Spirits to take his soul with care,' said Sacred Cloud, 'but what of Blue Bird?'

'We searched well, but found no trace of her, no tracks.' Wild Horse looked away. The chief had not given his lost daughter a single thought since they had caught sight of the bison. They hadn't searched well.

'You must keep trying.' Sacred Cloud tugged at Mogoll's arm.

'It's not your place to tell me what to do.' Mogoll shrugged her away.

Sacred Cloud stepped back. 'Blue Bird is your daughter, and she is lost somewhere, frightened and alone.'

The words hung in the air, as if waiting to be caught. *Frightened and alone.* They stung Wild Horse. Sacred Cloud was right: Blue Bird might be lost, or worse, attacked and eaten by wolves? How could she survive on her own?

'Of course we shall not give up hope,' he said.

The chief glared at him but Wild Horse did not look away.

'As the boy says,' Mogoll spoke at last, emphasising the word 'boy', 'we shall not give up hope. And we shall resume our search at sunrise. It will give Wild Horse a last chance to find Blue Bird and prove if he is worthy of becoming a husband for Night Rain.'

Bear Face squeezed Wild Horse's shoulder. He understood it was his father saying, *You must do this and not let me down.*

Wild Horse pictured Blue Bird standing on the ledge, outlined by the sun: *Please don't tell them you've found me.* Had he said the wrong thing? He hadn't expected Mogoll to say they'd resume the search, and he hoped that while they'd been at the Sacred Rock she had escaped, and was far away.

When they gathered round the campfires to eat, Mogoll asked Zuni to sit between himself and Night Rain. Wild Horse felt the glares of his father and Zuni grind into him, so he sat far from them. As he chewed the meat off a sloth bone, he wondered what Blue Bird was eating now – *if* she was eating.

He thought about snatching victory from Zuni by finding her. But that would lead him to winning a wife he did not want – Blue Bird had said she didn't have a sweet nature. He looked at Night Rain's heavy brow and dark eyes, her jaw as rigid as rock. Blue Bird must take after her mother; she had a softer face with a slightly pointed chin and eyes the colour of a ripening nut – not green, not quite brown. He was surprised that he'd noticed such detail. But he began to understand Blue Bird's bravery: it showed courage to leave her family and face the perils of the land on her own. If only he had the same courage.

Suddenly he yearned to disappear like Blue Bird. But he could not do it. He could not dishonour his father by running away. Wild Horse had to stay or the chiefdom would pass to Zuni. Sleep did not come easy.

Wild Horse crept out into the moonlight, strayed further and further from the camp. He found Blue Bird in the woodland. They laughed as they chased each other through the trees. She spun round, transformed into a sabretooth cat, her fangs bared . . .

Wild Horse woke, sweating. He tried not to fall back to sleep, but his eyelids drooped heavier and heavier.

. . . He raised his spear to kill the sabretooth, wanting to win Mogoll's test, but as he threw the spear the animal turned back into Blue Bird. She fell to the ground, dying. He cradled her in his arms, squeezed his eyes tight shut, opened them to find Night Rain taunting him . . .

The nightmare repeated through the night.

At sunrise he walked to the river to fill his water-skin. He was glad of the chill in the air until it reminded him of the night's rainfall. Night's rain. Night Rain.

Wild Horse shivered. If only he could win the test, but let Zuni take the wife. It was not possible. He had to choose whether to face the challenge like a man, to make his father proud, with the honour of winning Mogoll's daughter.

Or to run away, like a boy.

CHAPTER TEN

BLUE BIRD

A loud screech jolted Blue Bird awake in the middle of the night. All she could see was the dying embers of the fire glowing in the blackness of the cave. She lay there, waiting to hear the sound again.

At last the screech rang out again, and again.

Just the call of an owl.

She threw some wood on the fire and crawled to the entrance of the cave, where she listened to the sounds of the night: the gurgling river; the hushed whoosh of wings; leaves rustling in the breeze; the howl of a wolf. Stars twinkled in the dark sky, some tiny and dim, others burning bigger and brighter, a few flickering. Blue Bird didn't know which stars were which, but Sacred Cloud had told her that there was a star for each being that died, human and animal.

'*When you die, your soul flies up to the sky and turns into a star,*' her aunt had said, '*leaving your body for the other creatures that roam the land. One of the stars belongs to your mother.*'

From that moment Blue Bird had searched for her mother's star. As she gazed out of the cave, she was drawn to one that sparkled fitfully, a restless soul maybe. Perhaps this was her mother looking down; wanting to be with her, to guide her. It made Blue Bird feel less alone. She watched the stars until they started to fade and the sky grew lighter. Only then did she fall asleep, wrapped in her bearskin.

She didn't wake till past sunrise, her head full of dreams about stars fluttering through the sky like butterflies.

'But you can't eat butterflies,' she said to Paska, as she shared a piece of snake with her. 'That's enough for now. Hunting time.'

Paska might not understand all the words, but she understood her tone of voice. Blue Bird ran her hand along the dog's back. 'You're doing well. We could set off now, but if we stay one more sunset I'm sure together we could catch at least a rabbit and eat well tonight, with food to take with us for the day's walk.' It was a good plan. They'd have a morning of hunting and leave the cave tomorrow.

The low sun shimmered in the sky, though a breeze pushed along clouds, threatening to mask it. Blue Bird and

Paska made their way out of the cave and down towards the river. Paska was a little way ahead when Blue Bird saw her stop, crouch down, hackles rising.

Blue Bird froze as she looked across the water and saw what Paska had seen. She slowly slid to the ground and slithered behind a rock. Paska crept beside her.

Three sabretooths were lazing on a rocky outcrop on the other side of the river. Had they seen her? She wanted to run back to the cave, but knew the cats would surely come after her. She edged towards a cluster of bushes.

'Stay down, Paska,' she whispered.

Looking up to the sky, Blue Bird noticed the fast clouds were moving in her direction. The Spirits were helping her, sending her scent away from the three big cats. She and Paska crawled from rock to rock, bush to bush, using whatever cover they could find to get back to the cave; trying to keep the big cats in view without them seeing her.

Had the Spirits sent her the snake last night? If she hadn't caught that she might have crossed to the other side of the river in search of food, and in the darkness she would have been easy prey for the big cats.

As she clambered back up towards her cave Blue Bird could still make them out in the distance, smudges veiling the rocks. Such deadly smudges. She settled down behind a bush hiding her cave entrance.

Watching and waiting.

Blue Bird didn't dare miss any movements; she needed to know whether or not the cats crossed the river. Birds chattered around her, some of them flying low over the river, catching insects. Hunting for food, they reminded Blue Bird of what she should be doing. She looked up. Trees hung over the top of the big rock. If she climbed up, she would be unseen by the big cats but would still get a view of them – and she might find other places to hunt.

She glanced back. One of the sabretooths stretched and stood up. The others did the same. Her fingers tightened round her spear-shaft and she held her breath as the three beasts jumped down from the rocks and walked to the river. She watched them drink, willing them not to cross . . .

At last they loped away, skirting the edge of the woodland, before disappearing over the top of the ridge.

The danger had passed for her. But what of Wild Horse? Would he come back this way? Had the hunters seen the big cats? A tremor shook the whole of Blue Bird's body at the thought of Wild Horse being attacked by the sabretooths. But there was nothing she could do for him, so she asked the Spirits to keep him safe.

Now she had to hunt.

It looked like a strenuous climb to the top of the rock, so Blue Bird left Paska in the cave. She cut off two slices of the snake and put the remaining piece in the skin pouch where she kept the pemmican and nuts. She wrapped it tightly inside her sleeping-hide, so that Paska would not be tempted.

'Stay,' she said, biting into one slice of the meat and throwing the other to Paska. The dog grabbed the meat and lay down. Blue Bird knew she wouldn't move, except to alert her to danger.

She shuddered. So many dangers to face and she'd hardly started her long journey. She didn't even know where she was going! Was she brave or foolish?

She climbed up to the next ledge where she found another cave, smaller than hers, only waist high. There didn't seem to be anything inside it, and the ledge narrowed so she started climbing, scraping her fingers and bashing her knees against sharp edges as she scrambled to the top.

It was bordered with spindly trees and bushes as the top of the rock levelled, then dropped down sharply far on the other side to the scrubland below. In the distance she could see huge rocks like the one she was standing on, rows of rugged hills thrusting upwards against the skyline. Cedar scrub and cactus plants clutched the rough terrain. Was that the course she'd have to take?

She leant against a tree, listening to the chirps of the birds as they swooped and soared. Two rabbits, then a third and a fourth hopped into view and crouched, ears twitching, to nibble at the sparse grass. Three more joined them. The rabbits hadn't noticed Blue Bird, but up here they probably saw few predators. She pressed herself against the tree, and asked the Spirits to send them closer to her.

Her hand tightened on the spear. She'd aim for a clean hit, but would be content to injure one enough to slow down its escape. She could chase an injured rabbit, and kill it with her knife.

Gradually the rabbits moved closer and Blue Bird's

spear arm started to ache with the tension of keeping so still. Mogoll had taught her how to hold a spear and when to attack, but she knew she'd have to judge it perfectly. One false move and they'd run off before she took aim.

The rabbits scattered like a starburst as she threw the spear; it pierced the ear of one of the rabbits and the rabbit was too dazed to avoid her knife when she threw herself to the ground, arms outstretched.

Back at the cave Blue Bird sliced off another portion of snake for herself and Paska before setting to work. She cut off the feet, head and tail so that she could remove the skin in one piece; it might come in useful. After placing the rabbit over a hot stone in the fire to cook, she scraped the fat away from the skin and stretched it over a rock to dry. It wasn't the fattest of the rabbits she'd seen, but with the remains of the snake it was enough to start their journey with.

Cautiously, she clambered down to the river to fill her water-skin, Paska beside her. Now she needed to decide which direction to take when they set off at sunrise. Not following the course of the river towards the rising sun as she'd hoped – not yet – as that might lead her to Wild Horse's camp.

Across the bleak terrain then. Towards the hills. As she turned away from the river to confront it, Paska's low growl made her spin round.

In the distance, coming back down the slope, she could see those deadly smudges. The sabretooths had returned.

CHAPTER ELEVEN

WILD HORSE

'Time to set off,' shouted Mogoll as Wild Horse put spare points in the hunting pouch tied to his belt. 'Sacred Cloud thinks my lost daughter may follow the river towards the rising sun, towards this camp. We shall return to her tracks at the river, and hope that the Spirits guide us to her.'

Wild Horse cursed Sacred Cloud under his breath. Blue Bird's aunt didn't realise that her niece didn't want to be found – unless Blue Bird had changed her mind, but he doubted that.

The search party moved swiftly along the course of the river, but Wild Horse sensed that Mogoll wasn't expecting to find his daughter, and guessed his mind was on the bison feast planned for their return. The women were preparing the fire-pits as they left. And no doubt scraping clean the hide that Mogoll wanted for Night Rain and her new husband. Wild Horse didn't want to think about that.

They slowed as they drew closer to the place where Blue Bird's tracks had been seen. The woodland lay ahead of them.

Wild Horse felt the vibration first.

He looked up to the ridge he'd led them over the previous day, saw a blur of dust, and a large herd of deer dashing through it. And behind the herd, a sabretooth cat.

It raced into view, just as Wild Horse saw two more big cats hidden at the edge of the trees.

The first cat was sending the deer towards an ambush. Clever. He knew that sabretooths had powerful limbs to accelerate quickly, but they couldn't sustain the speed for long. The waiting predators would stay low and hidden until they could make a swift strike.

Zuni raised his head like a young stallion, drew back his lips: 'Cla-cla-cla.' It was the noise made with the tongue at the back of the throat, used by the hunters in their tribe to signal when they were close to a prey. A signal for everybody to ready their spears.

It forced Wild Horse to do the same, making the same *Cla-cla-cla* signal. Everybody gripped their spears. Though they would be returning to the bison feast, the tribesmen could not miss a chance to make another kill. They could take down a deer or two. *Or a sabretooth*, thought Wild Horse. They might be able to attack the big cats while they fed. That would surely impress Mogoll.

The two waiting sabretooths lunged at one deer that ran closer to the trees. It changed direction to escape them, moving towards the open ground, but it was tiring after the chase. Its body flew upwards as the first cat charged into it. As the deer fell to the ground any life left in it was punctured by the thrust of long fangs into its neck.

The hunters edged forward, eagerly.

'It is better to wait!' Wild Horse said.

'Why?' said Zuni, holding his spear aloft. 'Come, let's move.'

'We must work together,' Wild Horse hissed, 'and stay low, or we'll attract the attention of the sabretooths.'

'I'm not taking your orders, Wild Horse,' said Zuni. 'I remember what happened to Lightning because of you. The herd will scatter as it reaches the river. We can head it off and chase some animals into the trees. We're bound to make a kill.'

He took off with his men, closely followed by Great Wolf who said over his shoulder, 'I go with Zuni. He keeps showing he is the better hunter.'

Wild Horse felt Bear Face's gaze dart from him to Mogoll.

As he suspected, the lead sabretooth joined the other two big cats already tearing flesh from their kill. He knew that if all the hunters had stayed together this would have been their moment to slay a sabretooth. It hadn't occurred to Zuni – he had lost them that chance as he chased after deer with half the hunters. Now Wild Horse couldn't endanger the lives of his few men against three such large beasts.

'Zuni is a fool,' Tall Tree whispered so that only Wild Horse could hear.

'Maybe I'm the fool,' said Wild Horse. 'My cousin will return with a kill, leaving me here to watch. Zuni led his men well. They moved just in time. It is too late for us to follow them to the woodland – the big cats will see us now.'

'Do not doubt yourself, Wild Horse. Zuni was lucky to get across without the sabretooths seeing him. If he keeps taking risks like that he'll lose another man. That is not being a good leader. You will become a great leader.'

'It was Running Bear who wanted to be a great leader,' said Wild Horse. 'Not me.'

'Your brother was a good hunter, but he let Zuni goad him into actions that I warned him against. He was weak where you are strong.'

Wild Horse shook his head; he didn't want to believe that his brother had any weaknesses.

'Think how well you diverted the bison from trampling us,' added Tall Tree. 'You might not feel ready yet, but there will come a time when you'll know it is right for you to lead.'

It was the most Tall Tree had ever said to him. Wild Horse wasn't sure how to reply.

'It needed saying,' said Tall Tree.

Wild Horse looked at the sabretooths, saw how the lead female's belly bulged. This could be her last meal before she gave birth.

Bear Face, standing behind him with Mogoll, broke through his thoughts. 'Zuni is after the deer. This is your chance to make me proud. With the sabretooths distracted by their kill, your spears could take one.'

'Zuni shouldn't have left us,' said Wild Horse. 'We do not have enough hunters to attack three big cats. And there could be a male nearby.'

'Well, take them now,' ordered Mogoll, 'before the male arrives.'

'But we'd have to go into the open to get close enough to throw our spears,' argued Wild Horse. 'They'll see us and attack. We'll lose a man.'

'Are you afraid to die?' said the chief.

'No. I'm not afraid to die,' Wild Horse snarled.

'Then waste no more time,' said Mogoll, 'or maybe your father and I should show you what to do.'

Wild Horse glared at him. 'I know what to do. If someone has to die it should be me. It is a good time to die.'

Bear Face said, 'Do not fail me, Wild Horse.'

'You should take cover with Mogoll,' Tall Tree said to Bear Face. 'You will see how brave your son is.'

Wild Horse nodded thanks to Tall Tree; not just for the kind words, but for realising that Wild Horse did not want Bear Face with him for the attack.

'Mogoll has goaded you as Zuni did your brother,' Tall

Tree whispered as the chiefs drew back.

'I know, friend, but I had no choice, in front of my father,' said Wild Horse as he signalled to the hunters to follow him.

As ever, Tall Tree had his three spare spears. So did Wild Horse.

'May the Spirits guard us and guide us,' said Wild Horse as he led the hunters towards the gorging sabretooths.

The hunters murmured in agreement as they set off, moving quickly and stealthily between bushes and rocks. Wild Horse was the first to break cover. The predators were tearing flesh from bone as Wild Horse edged forward, his gaze darting from one cat to another. The closest one was the smallest and youngest; it should be the easiest to kill. The other two would be more wary.

In the seconds it took Wild Horse to glance across to the trees to check on Zuni, the sabretooths sensed the hunters.

They sprang up from their feast, and the men charged, spears raised, yelling. But the big cats did not run – and the youngest bounded towards them.

Wild Horse threw his spear, at the same time as Tall Tree lunged forwards with his – blocking Wild Horse's body with his own. Both spears hit their mark, but the animal did not stop. It leapt at Tall Tree, using the might of its upper body to wrestle him to the ground, where it delivered a deep stabbing bite through Tall Tree's neck. A savage but instant death.

With two spears already in its side, the big cat could not

avoid the spears thrown by the rest of Wild Horse's hunters. The other sabretooths turned and ran.

Wild Horse fell to his knees by Tall Tree's body. He could hear himself yowling like a wolf, and could barely breathe as he held his friend against his chest, yearning for some sign of life yet knowing that was impossible. How could this have happened? One moment Tall Tree was telling Bear Face he would see how brave his son was, the next he had given up his own life so that Wild Horse might live. It wasn't right. Wild Horse squeezed his eyes tightly shut, wanting to take Tall Tree's place. He had been ready to die. *He* should be lying here dead, in Tall Tree's arms.

He heard Mogoll call out that maybe they'd end up with another sabretooth kill, and opening his eyes he saw one of the big cats escaping up the ridge, though the pregnant female was running towards the trees where Zuni and his men were grouped around two deer carcasses.

'No,' screamed Wild Horse, jumping up as he saw Zuni take aim. *It would be a waste of another life, a life that should be allowed to bring forth more life.*

The female faltered, distracted by Wild Horse's call.

'Let her go,' shouted Wild Horse. 'She is ready to cub. Leave her to have young that we can hunt another day.'

Zuni would not be put off. His spear-point pierced the sabretooth's neck and she turned away, yelping, as the shaft broke off. Zuni set off after her as she raced into the woodland.

'There should be no honour in slaying an animal so

close to birthing,' Wild Horse cried out as he stumbled back to where Tall Tree lay. He gulped for air. His throat, his chest, his whole body felt dry. First Running Bear, now Tall Tree. He crouched by his friend's body.

Why? Why did you do that for me? I don't deserve it.

Zuni called out that they had lost the female, yelling that he would have brought down the big cat if it hadn't been for Wild Horse.

Bear Face strode towards him. 'Your foolish cry gave Zuni a better chance to take aim, and then blame you for his failure to make a kill.' Wild Horse hunched into his shoulders. 'You have brought dishonour to yourself and to me. And the animal might have escaped if you hadn't called out. It will lose much blood and suffer a slow, lingering end.'

Wild Horse couldn't bear to think he might be the cause of the animal's death, as well as the death of his friend. But Tall Tree had decided it was his time to die, not Wild Horse's – he had not realised how brave his friend had been until that moment. He stood and tried to lift Tall Tree's body – his spirit must fly up to join all other Spirits – but his knees buckled beneath him.

'Father, please . . .'

He couldn't believe he was asking for his father's help. But somehow it seemed right, that they should find a resting place for Tall Tree together. Bear Face had taken in Tall Tree as an orphan not long after Running Bear was born.

In silence, father and son carried the body of Tall Tree to a large flat rock by the river. They lifted him up and laid him on the top of the rock, where the Spirits could easily find his soul. And where the eagles and vultures, and maybe even the sabretooths, could find his body.

Silence fell between the two as they sat cross-legged either side of the body, deep in their own thoughts. As Bear Face thanked the Spirits for bringing Tall Tree to them, and for giving him a swift and honourable death, Wild Horse wanted to shout at the Spirits for allowing his friend such a violent and early death.

It should have been me who died, not Tall Tree – was all he could think. He suspected his father felt the same. At least then Bear Face could say his son had died with honour, instead of bringing more shame to the tribe.

Wild Horse stayed by the body when Bear Face walked back to the rest of the hunters. He looked up to the sky. Were there any Spirits up there, and if so, where were they when Tall Tree needed them?

'Come,' he heard Mogoll call, 'it is time to return to the camp. We have our champion.'

Wild Horse turned to see Zuni strutting towards the chief. *His* hunters had brought down two deer. *His* chance to kill a sabretooth had been ruined by Wild Horse. Wild Horse and his hunters had slain a sabretooth but they had lost a man. There was no honour in that.

Wild Horse didn't move, couldn't move. It was as if he had become part of the rock.

Mogoll shouted, 'I said "come", Wild Horse.'

'Do not cast more dishonour on me,' called Bear Face, his face severe, his eyes piercing and unyielding.

Wild Horse climbed down from the flat rock. 'What about the search?' he said. 'Have you forgotten we're meant to be looking for your daughter?'

In three strides Mogoll was upon Wild Horse. He swung his arm round with a blow to Wild Horse's head, knocking him to his knees. Wild Horse had sensed what was going to happen, could have defended himself, but he felt so wounded inside his body it was almost as if he needed some other hurt to hide the inner pain.

'I think we've all seen how treacherous this place is,' said Mogoll, raising his voice. 'How can one small girl survive against so many dangers, when with so many hunters we have lost a man?' He glared at Wild Horse. 'The sabretooths were not afraid of your hunters. It is likely that they have already taken the life of a human. I fear that life was Blue Bird's. I ask the Spirits that her departure was swift like Tall Tree's. She was brave in life, and I am sure would have been brave facing death.'

Wild Horse knew that he was the only person who might argue with the chief, but there was no fight left in him. Zuni and Dark Wolf each had a deer slung across their shoulders to carry back in triumph, and Mogoll's hunters had quickly gutted and quartered the sabretooth while Wild Horse and Bear Face had settled Tall Tree to rest.

'And we have something to celebrate.' Mogoll stretched his arms towards Zuni. 'I have found a brave hunter to take my daughter Night Rain as a wife.'

Zuni stretched his neck up like a condor, and looked

directly at Wild Horse, his eyes glinting with contempt. Wild Horse allowed his cousin's stare to add to the sickening sensation churning through him.

As he started to follow the hunters he looked back at the butchered carcass of the sabretooth and saw Tall Tree's spears. He ran to pick them up, holding them in his hands for some time. They needed to be placed beside Tall Tree, a sign to the Spirits that he was a true hunter.

As he said his last goodbye to his friend Wild Horse looked towards the rock face on the far side of the river, where he had climbed and found Blue Bird. If only she was still there; he knew she would understand.

But Mogoll was right. What chance did she have of surviving out here all alone?

CHAPTER TWELVE

BLUE BIRD

B lue Bird was glad that it wasn't Wild Horse who had died. Watching him place the spears next to the body of Tall Tree she could almost feel his grief across the river and wanted to call out to him. To comfort him. She struggled to stay silent.

She'd taken cover behind a low rock, flattening herself against it, as if that would fuse her into it, turn her into rock, so that she couldn't be found by the sabretooths. Then she'd realised that they didn't know she was there, that they had a different prey.

So she'd seen everything that had happened. A fear that Wild Horse had betrayed her and led Mogoll back here had turned into a fear that Wild Horse would be slain by the sabretooths. And when her father struck him she wanted to cry out. Wild Horse didn't deserve to suffer for reminding Mogoll about her.

Maybe if she stood up and said she was safe, that she would go back with them, Mogoll would realise Wild Horse had been right. But there seemed to be no sorrow in her father, no grief that she might be dead. *I ask the Spirits that her departure was swift . . .* He seemed more interested in Night Rain's new husband.

She slumped down. What should she do now?

She couldn't move. The sabretooths might return to the deer carcass now that the hunters had gone. So she waited and listened, Paska lying beside her, resting her chin on Blue Bird's thigh.

Sunlight soon began to fade – she needed to get back to the cave. She peered round the rock. Everywhere seemed calm, as if it had shrugged off the turmoil that had happened earlier. She scanned the other side of the river, from the woodland to the abandoned deer carcass – the sabretooths hadn't returned – and finally to the rock where Wild Horse had laid the dead hunter.

As her gaze settled on Tall Tree's resting place an idea jabbed at her. Was it wrong to steal from the dead? Who would know? Would the Spirits be angry?

'Or maybe,' she murmured to herself, 'it is the Spirits telling me to use my wits and make use of what I see.'

She decided it was a waste to leave good spears behind when she needed another so desperately. Ignoring a twinge in the back of her mind, the thought that Sacred Cloud might disapprove, she ran across the stepping stones and climbed on to the flat rock.

'I thank you, friend of Wild Horse,' she said as she leant over the body, her finger outlining the shape of a star on the forehead. 'Let this star help the Spirits find you.' She picked up three of the spears. 'I'll leave you the spear-shaft that helped bring down your killer. It is the one that proves your courage as a hunter.'

She hoped that would appease the Spirits, and tried not to feel so pleased. But earlier, when she'd been hunting the rabbits, she'd really wanted a spare spear. Now she had three.

The thoughts of the rabbit reminded her that she was hungry and thirsty, so she drank from her water-skin before topping it up from the river.

'Come, Paska, we must eat.'

But when they reached the bottom of the rock face, Paska stalled and tensed.

'What's wrong?' asked Blue Bird as she knelt by the dog. She put her hand on the ground and felt a tacky moistness. Blood. With darkness looming she hadn't seen it. 'The sabretooth,' she whispered, remembering the big cat running from the hunters with a spear-point in its neck. Had it come out of the woodland after the hunters had gone and crossed the river here? The safest thing was to get back to the cave and build a fire close to the cave entrance to ward off predators. But as she scrambled on to the ledge by her cave, a gasping sound made her freeze, her own breath quickening, a heavy pounding in her chest.

There was something in the cave.

She should get away. But all she had was in there. She slowly laid down Tall Tree's spears, keeping hold of her own as she crawled forwards on her hands and knees.

The gasps grew louder and Blue Bird stopped and listened, trying to control the sense of foreboding rising within her. They were gasps of suffering rather than growls of menace. She heard again Wild Horse's cries to Zuni, about there being no honour in killing an animal close to having her cubs. Had the sabretooth come to her cave to give birth? Or to die?

She had to find out.

Swallowing her fear, Blue Bird gripped her spear and edged towards the cave entrance. She peered in.

The big cat was lying on its side, blood from the gaping neck wound oozing over the floor of the cave. Beside her, one cub was struggling to find its mother's milk as another was battling to be born. Blue Bird had to get away before she was seen. Animal or human, Blue Bird knew that mothers attack if they fear a threat to their young.

A thunderous roar blasted towards her.

Too late . . .

Blue Bird tried to tighten the grip on her spear but found she couldn't flex her fingers. She was rigid with fear.

All courage had deserted her.

CHAPTER THIRTEEN

WILD HORSE

Wild Horse trailed behind the returning hunters, so that he did not have to witness any returning glory that might be showered upon Zuni. For a while he skulked behind the bushes and rocks that sheltered the camp. When he peered through the branches he saw Sacred Cloud pleading with Mogoll, who dismissed her with a flick of his arm. She wept and stumbled into the arms of Fawn.

Gradually everybody sat down around the two campfires, which sputtered with the tang of bison juices from the beasts cooking over them. There was much chatter and laughter.

'What are you doing out here, Wild Horse?' It was Little Bear, his youngest brother, who was just eight winters old. 'Aren't you joining us for the feast?'

Wild Horse turned to the boy. 'I'm not hungry, Little Bear. You go and join Grey Horse.'

'Come on.' The small boy grabbed his hand. 'I hope you're not staying away because Zuni won the contest to get the wife.'

'Wife.' Wild Horse let the word slither over his tongue, tainting his mouth with its bitter taste.

'She's bossy and lazy,' his brother said. 'She upset Mother today by not helping with the preparations. She said she was too busy braiding her hair and sewing feathers on to her best tunic. And her face is as sour as an unripe berry.'

Wild Horse allowed the boy to lead him to the feast where he caught sight of Night Rain. 'You are right, Little Bear,' he whispered, 'she does have a sulky look.' *No sign of sweetness; no flicker of a smile*, he thought. *Not like Blue Bird with her flashing eyes and ready grin.*

'Ah, here comes the loser,' Mogoll jibed. 'It is good you have joined us to celebrate.'

'We would have more to celebrate if somebody hadn't spoilt my chance to slay a sabretooth,' said Zuni. He put his hand to knife at his belt.

Little Bear tugged at Wild Horse's hand. It stopped him from seizing his own knife and attacking his cousin.

The regret of his own tribespeople gouged into him as Bear Face gave thanks to the Spirits for providing them with much good meat. Everybody raised their arms to praise the Spirits. Wild Horse didn't. He wanted to shout that there weren't any Spirits. If they existed, then Tall Tree would still be alive, and Running Bear too. Neither had deserved to die.

Wild Horse brooded as he devoured the meat. *The meat had come from the bison killed by Tall Tree and his band of hunters, not from the Spirits.* He was lost in thought when Mogoll stood up.

'Great Wolf and I have agreed that his son Zuni and my daughter Night Rain should be joined together. Zuni has shown he is a skilful hunter and leader. He is a worthy winner.'

Zuni's thin mouth slashed open into a *sneer*. A sneer that said, *It is right that you honour me. It is right that I win the wife.*

Wild Horse stood. He couldn't bear to listen to any more. Zuni didn't deserve the honour he was getting.

Bear Face hissed, 'Stay.'

'Let him go and lick his wounds of defeat,' said Zuni. 'He has suffered deeply.'

Wild Horse scanned the faces, looking for some support, willing Tall Tree's grin to appear. But there was no Tall Tree – never again would he see that face. Wild Horse felt a tear rip through his body. He wanted to escape from the looks of disapproval, but he couldn't bear to appear cowardly. What should he do?

A voice inside his head whispered, '*Don't let them goad you.*' Tall Tree was with him after all.

'I'm going nowhere.' He stood proud. 'I just wanted to say "well done" to my cousin. He deserves the prize. They are a good match.'

Yes, he thought, *Zuni deserves such a wife*. A wife with a face as sharp as his own. Night Rain's dark eyes caught Wild Horse's briefly, but she quickly looked away. For a moment he felt sorry for her – she didn't look particularly pleased at becoming Zuni's prized wife. He sat down and blocked out everything going on around him, working out what he was going to do.

Darkness fell. The children and mothers withdrew to their shelters. More wood was thrown on the fires. Those who remained drew closer, retelling hunting stories and ancient legends. The buzz of chatter hovered over the camp, as if keeping the storytellers safe.

Wild Horse slipped away. He pulled back the flap of the shelter he shared with his family. Both his brothers were asleep, and Wild Horse was relieved to hear his mother's gentle snoring. He would miss them deeply and they would miss him, but he knew he could not stay. He hoped they'd understand, that they wouldn't think him a coward. They might even be glad. Leaving would show he had the courage to survive on his own.

Working quickly, he collected his spear-points and fore-shafts, knife and water-skin, as well as his tools wrapped in their hide pouch. He rolled everything up in a camel sleeping-hide and secured the roll and his spears to a harness his mother had made from strips of sinew and hide. All his spears except the presentation one: that meant nothing to him now – it was part of his past.

When Little Bear stirred, Wild Horse flinched, but the boy turned over and slept on. Wild Horse reached out to touch his brother, and his hand lingered in mid-air. He took a deep breath, laid his presentation spear next to Grey Horse – as the older of the two it was right that he should have it.

'*Remember me,*' he whispered softly as he picked up the hide roll containing his belongings, '*and I'll always remember you.*' He left the shelter before he changed his mind. If Blue Bird was brave enough to leave her tribe, then so was he.

He skirted round the inner edge of the camp, catching snippets of tales. Bear Face was telling Mogoll the story of Running Bear defeating a ground sloth on his own; Zuni was relating his version of the encounter with the sabretooth cat to Night Rain; Grey Wolf was boasting about his son's hunting skills to anybody who'd listen.

There was no sign of Sacred Cloud. Wild Horse crept around the shelters set up by Mogoll's people, hoping he could find her without disturbing anybody. As he wondered which shelter was hers, whimpers whispered into Wild Horse's ears and he edged closer to the shelter which covered the cries.

He crouched down by the flap. 'Sacred Cloud, is that you?' he said softly.

The sobbing faltered.

'Sacred Cloud,' Wild Horse repeated, 'it is Wild Horse,

son of Bear Face, leader of one of the search parties to find Blue Bird. Can I . . . ?'

The shelter flap flew back before he could finish.

'Have you seen her?' Sacred Cloud wiped the tears with her hand. 'She isn't dead, is she? The Spirits tell me that she isn't dead, whatever Mogoll says.'

Wild Horse looked over his shoulder, fearful he might be seen.

Sacred Cloud tugged him through the open flap, which she pulled shut. The darkness shrouded them. 'You have seen her, haven't you? I could see from the way the moon glowed on your face.'

'Yes, I did see her. On the first search. I haven't seen her since.'

Sacred Cloud fell to her knees. 'Why didn't you bring her back? How could you leave her out there all alone?'

'Because she didn't *want* to come back. She made me promise not to tell anyone where she was. She told me that she'd run away because she was so unhappy.'

Sacred Cloud said nothing, but Wild Horse could hear her jagged breathing. 'Blue Bird often asked me about her mother, and where our tribe came from,' she said at last. 'It is too far. She will never find it.'

'But you have told her which stars you would follow, which rivers and mountains to pass, and to walk towards the sunrise,' said Wild Horse.

'Oh, Wild Horse, like her you have no idea what a journey it would be.'

'Blue Bird said that you had great faith in the Spirits,

and so does she.'

'I fear, even with the Spirits' guidance, that I could not find my way back. If I'd known that Blue Bird wanted to go on such a journey I would have told her it was impossible.'

'Tell me what you have told Blue Bird,' said Wild Horse. 'If I find her again, I'll help her.'

'What about your family? You belong here.'

'Not any more. Like Blue Bird, I too am unhappy.'

Sacred Cloud clasped her hands. 'I am sad for you, but glad for Blue Bird. At least she won't be alone. But how will I know if you've found her, if she is still alive?'

Wild Horse shrugged his shoulders in the darkness. 'You say your Spirits told you she is not dead, so you must believe that they will let you know if I find her.'

'Yes, you are right. They will send me a sign. I will tell you what I remember . . .'

It was very late when Wild Horse crept out of Sacred Cloud's shelter. He made his way to the edge of the camp. There were only a few people left around the campfires – he would not be seen as he crept away.

'What are you doing?'

Wild Horse swung round. His father came towards him, frowning. 'Walking,' said Wild Horse, 'and wondering how I can make you proud of me.'

'And how can you?'

Images of Tall Tree and the injured sabretooth forced their way into Wild Horse's head. Too much shame. Silence yawned like the gaping mouth of a crocodile; Wild Horse felt that he might fall into it and be lost.

'Why are you carrying that?' Bear Face pointed at the hide roll on his back.

'I have decided that I will go into the wilderness on my own. I shall learn to survive against whatever creatures and storms cross my path. Many nights under the stars will make a man of me, a man to make any father proud. So that one day I can return with honour.' Wild Horse didn't know where he found such words, but he felt better for having said them. He wasn't sure if his father would accuse him of running away like a coward.

But Bear Face nodded. 'You are right to leave. There is no honour if you stay here.'

So his father was letting him go.

'Chert,' said Bear Face, thrusting a piece of flint into Wild Horse's hand. 'Mogoll traded it for our dried meats and berries. You should be able to make at least two good points if you flake it carefully.'

'Thank you, Father. It is a fine gift.'

'It is not a gift. It is a tool to help you gain your manhood. Do not come back unless you are sure you can make me proud.'

Wild Horse curled his fingers around the chert before placing it in the pouch attached to his belt. He didn't know what to say.

Bear Face said, 'The Spirits go with you.' And before Wild Horse could say anything, he strode back to the fire.

Wild Horse unfastened one of his spears to carry, ready for what the night might bring. He did not look back as he set off. Instead, he gazed at the stars as Blue Bird would have done, a sense of freedom flowing through him. He wondered if she was gazing at them now. Would he find her again and help her find her mother's tribe as he'd promised Sacred Cloud? Or was she already lost?

CHAPTER FOURTEEN

BLUE BIRD

It happened so quickly, yet seemed as slow as a bud unfurling: the roar of the sabretooth defending her newborns; the fear that the mother cat would find enough strength to attack, no matter how bad her injuries; Paska leaping to Blue Bird's side – *ready to die for her or with her*.

If it hadn't been for Paska nudging her, Blue Bird might not have found the strength to leap down to the ledge below. She gazed up at the rock face, then down to the river – the other sabretooths might pick up their scent there. Darkness was falling, so it would be difficult to find a refuge, but she remembered the small cave she'd discovered and decided she'd feel safer above where the sabretooth lay with her cubs than in any shelter below. And from up there it would be easier, come sunrise, to climb to the top of the rock and work out her escape.

If she survived until sunrise.

With trembling hands Blue Bird scrambled up the rock face and along narrow ledges that led to the cave – ledges that might be too narrow for a large injured sabretooth.

Or maybe not too narrow for a sabretooth which needed to eat, to gain strength to feed her cubs? The deer kill was probably meant to be her last before giving birth. That had been denied her, and a desperately hungry sabretooth might well be able to cling on to the ledge. Blue Bird tried to tell herself that the cat was too weak from the birth and too badly injured to move. She'd seen much blood.

She shook the image out of her head as she crawled into the cave. It wasn't big enough to stand up in, but was deep enough for Blue Bird to lie down with Paska by her side. As she curled around the dog for warmth she thought of all her belongings trapped in the cave below with the sabretooth – and shivered as she pictured being wrapped in her bearskin, a flickering fire for warmth and protection. She blinked away images of the rabbit and snake, which the cat had probably eaten. But that might be a good thing, she reasoned – the cat would be less hungry, less likely to leave her cubs and go hunting.

And what about the pemmican and the fire-stones, her

bone needles, Sacred Cloud's balm? And Tall Tree's spears left on the ledge? She was down to just one spear again. At least she had a water-skin and the hunting pouch tied to her belt.

Blue Bird closed her eyes and whispered to the Spirits, 'Thank you for delivering us from the mouth of the sabretooth. Please send your guidance to help us through the night.'

A picture of Paska's puppies suckling at their mother's teats floated behind Blue Bird's closed eyelids. Was this the guidance she had asked for? She opened her eyes and sat up. Should she follow the signs sent by the Spirits? Had Paska's milk dried up?

Gently she massaged the dog's teats – drops dampened her fingers. It seemed to bring relief to Paska, as if the milk needed to be released, and Blue Bird licked her fingers, finding comfort in the warm richness. She repeated the process, some for herself and some for Paska.

Soothed by the milk Blue Bird snuggled up to Paska in search of sleep. But each time she drifted towards slumber the sabretooth roared, its eyes cutting through her closed eyelids. It prowled the cave beneath her, did not let her forget she was not alone on this rock. It would climb up and seize Paska and Blue Bird with those long fangs. She clasped Paska close to her.

The sun had not yet crept into the sky when she crawled out of the cave, but darkness was receding. She stretched her arms to thank the Spirits for keeping her safe – so far. Now she had to decide whether to climb to the top of the rock, or to go down to her cave.

Deep inside she already knew what she was going to do. Even though the sabretooth might be waiting, she had to return to the cave. To tackle the long journey to find her mother's tribe without her belongings seemed far worse than facing the cat. And most important, she must find her mother's rabbit-skin pouch and Sacred Cloud's balm. She vowed to herself that if she found them, she would for ever keep them in her hunting pouch. She could collect Tall Tree's spears, too, then she'd have four spears with which to defend herself from attack. And this time she wouldn't turn into stone filled with terror. She knew what she was going to face.

The air was still, yet Blue Bird knew that all the mother cat's senses would be alert to any danger to her new cubs. She had to be as quiet as a cloud hanging in the sky.

She paused as she reached the ledge leading to her cave. With one jab of her finger she signalled to Paska to go no further. She stood there, waiting, listening. A quiet mewing crept into her ears.

Blue Bird clutched her spear and looked into the cave, barely breathing. Through the dark shadows she could see that the sabretooth mother had clearly died, and two cubs lay still next to her. A third was trying to suckle.

Before she considered what she was doing, Blue Bird was beside the suckling cub, Paska at her side. She offered the cub to Paska and the dog instinctively lay down for the cub to suckle. It was as if that was what Blue Bird had seen when she had asked the Spirits for guidance – that was why Paska's milk hadn't dried up.

The cub backed off, its wobbly legs leading it back to its mother. Blue Bird reached for her knife and tore into the underbelly of the dead cat, removing a section of skin which she then rubbed on Paska's belly. 'Now, little one' – she lifted the cub and placed it back next to Paska's teats – 'that should help Paska to smell like your mother.'

It took several attempts, but Blue Bird persisted. She was sure that the Spirits had guided her to save this cub.

At last the cub started to suck hard and Paska's milk started to flow. Blue Bird felt her eyes fill with tears. Poor Paska had been denied the chance to be a mother to her own pups, but now she could help this cub.

Blue Bird made sure the two animals had settled in their new roles before making sure the other two cubs were dead, not just sleeping. Then she moved to the back of the cave to check on her belongings. The sabretooth had eaten the remains of the snake and the rabbit – she wondered if it had liked the taste of cooked meat.

She was relieved to find her bearskin, and allowed herself just one mouthful of pemmican. Paska would need food too, she thought, especially as she now had a cub to feed. She looked at the dead mother cat and the cubs – a plentiful supply of meat.

Leaving Paska and the orphan cub, Blue Bird stepped out of the cave to breathe in the fresh dewy air. She watched the dark sky lift to welcome shafts of light, felt her troubles drifting away.

She had survived the immediate danger. She was alive!

Paska was alive! She thanked the Spirits; today would be a good day.

From her vantage point on the ledge a flicker of movement on the far side of the river caught her attention and she watched a figure step down from the flat rock where the dead hunter lay, pause, then cross the river over the stepping stones.

Who was this intruder?

The figure drew closer, his pace quickening, and Blue Bird realised it was the boy, Wild Horse. Not boy perhaps, but not quite a man either: Wild Horse, the 'man-boy'. She wasn't sure why she was pleased to see him; perhaps it was because she'd felt his sorrow at losing Tall Tree. She was about to scramble down to the river and call his name when she saw another figure, following him.

CHAPTER FIFTEEN

WILD HORSE

Wild Horse walked slowly at first, partly because the clouds in the sky shrouded the moon and partly because the clouds in his head blurred his thoughts. So much had happened since the sun had risen, and now he was leaving everything he knew behind, not knowing if his father ever expected him to return. He tried to unravel Bear Face's last words in his head, but the knots just got tighter, so he concentrated on listening for creatures of the night. His head twitched every time he heard an unfamiliar sound. He walked and walked, without really knowing where he was going.

Eventually he realised where he was – the rock where

they'd laid Tall Tree's body. He had been drawn to his friend's final resting place, felt a need to say one final goodbye. He climbed up on to the flat rock, gazed at his friend's face, was glad to see no predators had yet found the body. There were richer pickings nearby; the remains of the earlier kills.

But only one of Tall Tree's four spears remained. Wild Horse couldn't imagine an animal running off with one spear, let alone three. Climbing back down the rocks he checked that they hadn't fallen, but they were gone. There were no signs of other hunters passing. 'Blue Bird,' he whispered into the breeze blowing the clouds across the sky as darkness ebbed away.

Wild Horse felt his mood lift. He'd only met Blue Bird once, and so far her disappearance had caused him nothing but difficulty. He wanted to feel angry that she'd taken the spears left to honour Tall Tree, but it was wise – the dead can't use spears.

He saw the wide flat stones spanning the river and guessed that was where she'd crossed, so he did the same. His pace quickened as he made his way to the rock face where he'd first seen her. Thoughts flashed through his mind. Had Blue Bird seen what had happened, but stayed hidden? If so, it proved how strongly she felt about not being found. He had been right not to reveal where she was.

When he reached the foot of the rock, below where he had first stood with Blue Bird, he saw dark-red splodges splattered over the ground. He yanked the hide roll off his shoulders, knelt down and dabbed his fingers over them.

Blood.

'Oh, Blue Bird, what has happened?' he called out. He traced the blood to the edge of the river, and a nightmare scene of Blue Bird being attacked and hurt crashed into his head. There was no body, no remains, so she might have made it to the river, and her body been carried away. Or maybe she hadn't been too badly injured and had managed to swim. If she could swim...

It was as he was gazing downriver that a sudden force knocked him off his feet and pinned him to the ground.

'So you know where the lost daughter is.' Zuni held his knife at Wild Horse's throat. 'You cried out her name as if you know her.'

'Of course I don't know her.' Wild Horse struggled, but he'd landed badly and his shoulder throbbed from the pain of Zuni kneeling on it. 'Why are you here, Zuni? Shouldn't you be with Mogoll, wolfing down the success of winning the wife?'

'I saw you leaving, and wanted to make sure you didn't weaken and return. I wasn't surprised you came back to Tall Tree's resting place, but I did wonder why you crossed the river.'

'Why shouldn't I cross the river? It doesn't mean I know where the girl is. Let me leave in the disgrace you wanted for me while you go back to your glory.'

Zuni shoved his knee further into Wild Horse's shoulder. 'Your cry to the girl sounded like you've seen her before. Finding her will bring me further honour. Tell me what you know and you'll live to see me take her back.'

'I've nothing to tell you.' Wild Horse wriggled in desperation.

'So you want to die?'

'You won't kill me. How would you explain my death?'

Zuni circled the knife round Wild Horse's neck. 'There will be no explaining,' he said. 'You've run away. All I need to do is let rumour spread, about you being too ashamed to stay. Even your own father was happy to see you go. In fact, I'll have that fine piece of chert he gave you.'

Wild Horse stared at his cousin, trying to work out how much he knew. If Zuni had watched him with Bear Face, had he also seen Wild Horse come out of Sacred Cloud's shelter? Had he led Zuni to Blue Bird? If she was still alive he couldn't risk Zuni finding her.

'Kill me or fight me fairly,' he said, gazing into Zuni's wild eyes – eyes which rolled back as Zuni's body suddenly jerked and slumped on to Wild Horse.

A boulder rolled by his side.

'That was one of my best throws.' Blue Bird was running towards him. 'Are you all right, Wild Horse?'

Wild Horse looked up at her. One moment he'd been filled with dread that Blue Bird had been savaged by the sabretooth, the next she was standing in front of him very much alive. Relief flushed away his fears, but as he pulled himself out from under Zuni's still body it became mixed with another dread.

'I think he's dead,' he said. 'And it could've been me.'

'Have you forgotten what a good shot I am?' Blue Bird

frowned at him. 'Remember the last time I threw something? It cast your spear aside.'

'But you've killed my cousin!' he said.

'Who was going to kill you. I thought you'd be pleased that I saved your life.'

'He was just threatening me to find out if I knew where you were. Zuni can be brutal when he kills animals, but he's never killed a man.'

'Well, it didn't look like *just* a threat to me.'

'Why would he kill me? I was no good to him dead.'

'And were you about to tell him something with that knife at your throat?' Blue Bird dropped to her knees beside the body. 'If you'd been as good a hunter and tracker as you think you are, you'd have known you were being followed and it wouldn't have been up to me to rescue you.'

'Like you, I didn't need rescuing,' said Wild Horse, cursing himself for not sensing Zuni behind him. 'I wasn't going to tell him anything. I didn't even know you'd still be here.'

'Now I see how ungrateful you are I wish I hadn't bothered. I'll leave you and your cousin.'

But as she turned to go, Zuni stirred and moaned. Blue Bird paused, frowning.

'It seems I didn't kill him after all,' she said. 'I suppose if the Spirits have saved him we should help.'

CHAPTER SIXTEEN

WILD HORSE

Blue Bird reached for the water-skin tied to her belt. 'I'll fill this – you decide what to do with him.'

As she stamped towards the river Wild Horse looked at the wound on Zuni's head, wondering if he should let him die, or maybe help him die.

Twice he picked up a boulder, thinking how easy it would be to crash it on to Zuni's head, and twice he put it down – there was no honour in killing a hunter so defenceless.

But there had been much hatred in Zuni's eyes when he held the knife at Wild Horse's throat. The more he thought about it, the more he thought Blue Bird was right and his cousin might have killed him if she hadn't thrown the boulder. Maybe it wasn't too late to finish him off.

'Is he still alive?' Blue Bird was suddenly by his side again.

'He's bleeding badly from this wound on his head.' Wild Horse was relieved not to be alone with his thoughts. 'But he breathes heavy.'

'A pity he didn't breathe heavy when he crept up on you.'

Wild Horse looked back to where he'd dropped his belongings, remembering the moments before being attacked by Zuni. About finding the blood, which he'd feared was Blue Bird's, but clearly wasn't. Whose was it? Did she know how close she'd been to danger?

Blue Bird dribbled water over Zuni's wound, and a little round his mouth. There was no response. Wild Horse grabbed the water-skin and poured the contents over Zuni's face. The eyes opened, then closed. So did the mouth and Zuni grunted as he tried to lift his head, tried to speak. His eyelids flickered as if trying to focus on the two figures leaning over him then his head flopped down again, eyes shut.

'What happens now?' asked Blue Bird.

'I don't know.'

'I'm going to have to leave straight away, because if he wakes up and sees me he'll go back to your tribe and tell my father that he knows where I am.'

'I thought you'd have gone by now.'

'So why did you come looking for me?'

Wild Horse sighed. 'I decided to leave my tribe too. And Blue Bird, I went to see your aunt before I left.'

'Sacred Cloud? Is she all right?'

'She was worried about you and angry with Mogoll for not finding you. I thought if I told her that I'd seen you alive it might make her less sad.'

'That was . . . kind of you.'

'She asked me to help you find your mother's tribe. She told me about the stars and the mountains and rivers.'

'That sounds like Sacred Cloud,' said Blue Bird, 'but I don't need any help, especially from someone who brings so much trouble with him.'

'I'm not offering to help. I'm just telling you what your aunt said.' Wild Horse clenched his fists. She was right; he had brought trouble with him. But he hadn't expected to be followed, hadn't considered that winning the challenge to take the wife would leave Zuni craving greater honour. And Zuni would soon realise Blue Bird was alive, for who else could have thrown that boulder?

Blue Bird continued, 'Your cousin will have a sore head and be angry when he wakes. And he'll need help to get him back to your tribe. It's your fault that he's here, so I'll pack up and leave and you can take him back.'

'I'm not going back. I told you, I've left.'

'Well, you can leave again after you've returned your cousin . . .'

They continued arguing until a voice moaned, 'My head. What happened? Where am I?'

Wild Horse and Blue Bird looked at each other.

'I hit you with a boulder because you were about to slit your cousin's throat, but sadly I didn't hit you hard enough,' said Blue Bird.

Zuni scowled and tried to sit up, grimacing as he clutched his head. 'My head feels like a herd of bison is charging through it. Who are you?' His eyes narrowed as he worked it out. He was no fool. Who else could she be? Zuni suddenly grabbed the knife still lying by his side where it had fallen and swung round, jabbing the weapon at Blue Bird.

With a low snarl, Paska rushed towards them and wrapped her jaw round Zuni's arm, making him scream and drop the knife. Wild Horse seized it.

Blue Bird took her time before she called off Paska. 'You shouldn't have done that, cousin of Wild Horse. You have just proved that I was right about you, and that it's a shame I didn't kill you with that boulder.'

'You're just a girl. You won't kill me.' Zuni squeezed his arm to stem the flow of blood.

Blue Bird took a knife from her pouch.

'What are you doing?' asked Wild Horse.

'Isn't it obvious? We have to kill him before he kills either of us. He is vermin.' Blue Bird's voice grew shrill, her eyes darting from Zuni to Wild Horse.

Wild Horse wasn't a coward and didn't want Blue Bird to think he was, but there was no honour in this.

'What about the Spirits?' he said.

Terror filled her eyes as she brandished the knife, her hand shaking. 'What about them?'

'Will they be pleased if you take Zuni's life?' He watched Blue Bird falter. 'Maybe we should let the Spirits decide whether or not to let him die, whether to let him be food for the animals or to send out a search party to save him.'

'How should we do that?' Blue Bird's hand stopped trembling.

'We tie him up and leave him here. There are many predators that like the taste of vermin.'

Blue Bird slowly loosened the grip on her knife. 'I ask the Spirits to do the right thing.'

Wild Horse took a length of sinew attached to the belt tied round the waist of his tunic and very quickly bound Zuni's wrists and ankles together. Zuni struggled at first, but stayed still when Blue Bird threatened to set the dog on him again.

'I forgot the cub.' She jumped up.

'What?' Wild Horse looked at her.

'I'll explain later. You stay here and watch him. I won't be long. Come, Paska.'

Before Wild Horse could say any more Blue Bird was gone.

'So my cousin now takes orders from a girl,' Zuni sneered.

'I'm not taking orders from anyone,' said Wild Horse.

'*You stay here and watch him.*' Zuni mimicked Blue Bird's voice. 'Sounds like an order to me, so that she can run off with that dog. You won't see her again.'

'She'll come back. You wait.'

'I can wait. I'm going nowhere.' Zuni held out his bound hands. 'But can you?'

Wild Horse walked back and forth between the river and Zuni, uncertainty scratching his skin. *Why had Blue Bird left so suddenly? What was there to explain about a cub?* He tried to tell himself that she'd soon be back.

But after much pacing there was no sign of her.

'It's not too late to go after her.' Zuni cut through his thoughts.

'What?'

'The girl. It's been some time since she left . . .'

'She hasn't run off. She's coming back,' Wild Horse said loudly.

'I hear the doubt in your voice, cousin. The doubt of a coward. Go now, find your guts. Find the girl and bring her back here. If you untie me I can be ready with a spear to kill the dog. We will return to the tribe with the prize of Mogoll's daughter. That will give you the honour you crave.'

'It's you who craves honour, not me.'

Wild Horse clutched his knife as he strode to the river to get away from Zuni. He searched the rock face. Where was Blue Bird? What was she doing?

'What about Bear Face's honour, Wild Horse?' he heard Zuni call. 'I know he wishes his son will return to him as a man he can respect. And I know how you can earn that respect.'

'You know nothing of my father.'

'I know that he wants what every father wants. For his son to achieve manhood, to make him proud.'

'If you know so much you'll know that he doesn't want me to return.'

'I know that you have brought great dishonour to Bear Face,' Zuni went on, 'and that is why he was glad for you to leave, but I think we both know what would change his mind . . .'

Honour!' yelled Wild Horse. 'You talk of honour, yet you know nothing of it. And you know nothing of me.' He ran back to Zuni and jerked his knife at him. 'I would feel no honour by capturing Blue Bird and returning her to her father. I would feel nothing but *shame*. Even if you are right and she has already flown, I will not untie you. I will leave you here to rot.'

He stared at Zuni, almost hoping that Blue Bird had set off. His breath quickened as the knife in his hand drew closer to Zuni's neck.

'You will not end my life, Wild Horse. It would bring even greater dishonour to you and to Bear Face.' Zuni bared his teeth like a trapped coyote.

Wild Horse tightened the grip on his knife to steady his hand. *Would taking his cousin's life cause him more dishonour?* Perhaps it would be worth it. This was his chance to be rid of Zuni.

They glared at each other, unaware of all other sights and sounds.

'Are you any good at butchering, Wild Horse?' Blue Bird's voice jolted him. She ran towards him.

'Butchering?' *Did she know what he was about to do? Was she expecting him to kill Zuni?*

'Butchering enough meat off a sabretooth for us to start the journey – if you're sure you want to leave with me.'

Wild Horse didn't need to think about it. 'I will leave with you,' he said, shaking the vision of slicing through Zuni's neck from his mind. 'But what did you mean about a cub?'

'I have saved a cub, a newborn, and Paska is its new mother. The real mother lies dead in my cave.'

Wild Horse shook his head. 'The injured sabretooth? What happened?'

'There is no time to tell you now,' said Blue Bird. 'We need to move fast. You go while I guard the vermin . . .'

Wild Horse climbed up to the cave and gasped at the sight of the dead cat sprawled across the floor of the cave.

As he started cutting into the animal's carcass he couldn't chase off the image of it running towards Zuni, full of life.

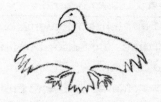

CHAPTER SEVENTEEN

BLUE BIRD

When Blue Bird had clambered up to the cave, listening for whimpering, she'd heard none; hoped the cub was asleep, but could see no sign of it. Fearing it had crawled out of the cave and fallen off the ledge, she'd peered over the edge. It was not there either.

But Paska had sniffed at the remains of the two dead newborns, and found the orphan nestled beside them. She had picked it up by its scruff and settled at the side of the cave to feed it.

It seemed that Wild Horse would be starting the journey with her. So she wouldn't be alone. Not that she felt alone with Paska and the cub for company.

She looked at the dead sabretooth – too much meat to waste. They should take some, would need food for the journey to help them get as far away as possible before nightfall, to leave Zuni far behind.

She'd packed up all her belongings by the time the cub had finished feeding. She decided to use the dried rabbit skin as a sling to carry it.

Vultures hovered over Tall Tree's resting place as she moved out of the cave, their dark shapes soaring and swooping. She looked down at the two hunters – they seemed to be talking.

There was something about it that unsettled her. Had she been so long in the cave that Zuni had convinced his cousin to betray her? Maybe the blood tie between them was too strong for Wild Horse to ignore? Maybe that was why he didn't want to kill Zuni – nothing to do with letting the Spirits make the decision.

Blue Bird checked her knife was back in the pouch tied to her belt, just in case, then heaved her hide roll on to her back, clutching the cub to her chest in the sling. She climbed down, careful not to be seen and laid down the cub next to her hide roll, hidden behind a large boulder.

Finally she got close enough to listen to what was being said, saw that Wild Horse was about to do what he'd stopped her from doing. She knew she couldn't let him end his cousin's life.

And now she was alone with Zuni.

He didn't know how lucky he was. With the right

command Paska could have inflicted a worse injury than she did. Blue Bird could have killed him, Wild Horse could have killed him.

Maybe it was right that they'd stopped each other. If she'd been standing here now with Zuni dead, her knife in his throat, would she be asking for forgiveness from the Spirits? If it wasn't his time to die when she threw the boulder – the Spirits had let him live – then it wasn't her right to take his life.

She considered what might happen if Zuni was rescued and married her sister. Night Rain was Mogoll's favourite daughter, and he would expect her husband to prize her as much as he did. Blue Bird pictured Zuni running round after Night Rain, trying to please her, for she would threaten him with Mogoll's wrath if he did not. The vision made her smile. Night Rain would make Zuni a fine wife, a wife he deserved.

'What are you grinning at?' Zuni snapped Blue Bird's thread.

She said nothing; didn't want to be drawn into talking.

'So you're too much of a coward to even answer my question. I knew you were just a frightened girl.'

'I'm not a coward and I'm not frightened.'

'So tell me what thoughts brought that grin to your face.'

'I was picturing your life with my sister. You have no idea how she expects to be treated, or how my father expects her husband to treat her.'

'My wife will be treated as I choose. She will answer to

me, not to her father.'

Blue Bird smirked. 'Night Rain will not be a quiet wife. Maybe I should kill you to save you.'

'And you have no idea what lies ahead of you. I will come after you. I will find you, unless . . .'

'Unless what?'

'You have shown strength, daughter of Mogoll. If I return with you and tell Mogoll of your courage he will honour us both.'

'I don't want my father's honour.' Blue Bird shivered.

'Yes, you do. We all want that. Untie me. Between us we can overpower my cowardly cousin and . . .'

'You are worse than vermin,' Blue Bird yelled, 'I will leave you here to perish and be eaten by the other vermin.'

'You will suffer if you leave me like this. Remember that.'

Blue Bird could almost taste the venom he spat at her. Her rage returned, and she drew her knife and stepped towards him.

Zuni glared at her. 'You don't have the stomach to use that knife on me. You know that if you kill me, my father will hunt you down. My death will be avenged.'

'My stomach tells me to use this knife . . .'

'What's happened?' Wild Horse hurried towards her.

Blue Bird clenched the knife. 'He threatened me. If we let him live, he will come after us.'

Wild Horse gripped her trembling shoulder. 'Zuni does to you what he did to me. He goads you. He does it well. He did it to my brother.'

'You praise me, cousin.' Zuni laughed. 'As did your brother. Running Bear couldn't resist the lure of a good kill. And the more I told him an animal was too dangerous the more determined he was to show off his daring.'

Wild Horse's voice was quiet as he said, 'Is that what happened the day he died?'

'He knew the bear was enraged. I told him so. I told him he'd lose if he attacked it,' said Zuni, 'but he wanted to prove me wrong.'

'And you didn't stop him,' said Blue Bird. 'You let him go to a certain death. All the more reason to be rid of you now – revenge for the loss of Running Bear.'

'It is not the time for revenge.' Wild Horse pulled Blue Bird away, but she could feel his arm trembling. He lowered his voice. 'We must stay strong and leave him. We must not let him win.'

'Your brother never ignored me,' shouted Zuni. 'You should not ignore me.'

'Don't think I don't want my cousin dead,' Wild Horse muttered to Blue Bird, 'but it is no honour to slay a hunter who is injured and bound. And if there comes a time when he should be dead, it should be at my hands, not yours. Let us leave him and you can be at peace with the Spirits.'

'What about his threat to come after me, to come after us?'

'Zuni is full of threats, but the thing he craves most is praise. If he gets back to the tribe he'll brag that he survived a vicious attack, *and* discovered that you live, making him even more worthy of taking a wife. He will forget about us.'

'At least that would mean Sacred Cloud knows I'm still alive,' said Blue Bird with a quiver of delight. 'Alive and strong.'

She walked to where she'd hidden the cub and her belongings.

'What's that?' asked Wild Horse, following her.

'The cub I saved.'

Wild Horse frowned. 'It's too weak to survive. I think it might be kinder to give it an easy death now.'

'No,' said Blue Bird as she pulled the sling across her shoulder and clutched the cub to her chest, 'it comes with us.'

'It will make our journey more difficult.'

'It's very small.'

'It will grow,' said Wild Horse, 'and get bigger and heavier.'

'But you said it wouldn't survive.'

'If it does . . .'

'By then it won't need carrying.'

'It will still need feeding.'

'Paska will take care of that until it is ready to be weaned. We can share our meat, and train it to hunt.'

'Blue Bird, sabretooth cats belong in the wild. How can we teach it to hunt? If it hadn't been for you it would be dead. It is not for us to interfere with the order of life.'

'How dare you say that?' Blue Bird snarled. 'We are taught to value the life of an animal heavy with young. If it hadn't been for you and Zuni, the mother cat would still be alive. So don't talk to me about interfering.' Blue Bird stroked the cub's head. 'It managed to survive the night its mother died, so it deserves a chance to live. I also want to give Paska the chance to be a mother. Have you forgotten what I told you about Burning Fire drowning her pups?'

Wild Horse said, 'No, of course not.'

'I didn't ask you to join me. If you don't like me having the cub it is best you go your own way.' Blue Bird glared at Wild Horse. An awkward silence hung over them.

Wild Horse nodded, 'I told Sacred Cloud I'd go with you. I'll be true to my word.'

Blue Bird signalled to Paska and started walking.

'You can't leave me like this,' Zuni shouted, 'The Spirits will be angered, and so will my father. Loosen my bonds or beware what harshness will follow you.'

Blue Bird kept walking, but Wild Horse stepped towards his cousin. He threw Zuni's spear across the river so that it landed in the scrub far on the other bank. 'I could have killed you, maybe should have killed you. Instead I leave you to writhe like the snake you are to free yourself and get your spear.' Leaning closer to Zuni he added, 'The Spirits will see I have shown you some mercy, cousin. But I will not forget you – if you ever threaten Blue Bird again you will regret it.'

Blue Bird felt a tingle of surprise; she hadn't expected such words from Wild Horse.

'Strange mercy when you know the vultures will smell my blood,' said Zuni to Wild Horse as he walked away, 'but it is you who will suffer. You will regret leaving me like this. I'm not frightened of you, Wild Horse. You'll never be the man your brother was'

Blue Bird watched Wild Horse come to an abrupt halt. She wondered what he was going to do, was relieved when he started walking again. He continued past her, saying nothing.

With a sense of freedom coursing through her, she patted Paska and checked the cub was snuggled in the sling. It was so small and vulnerable. Its mottled fur had been licked clean by Paska and the toothless mouth that would one day frighten foes with its deadly fangs had gently suckled at Paska's teats. She wanted to enjoy this moment. She had chosen to save the cub, and wanted to make sure it wasn't in vain.

As she set off after Wild Horse Zuni yelled, 'One day I will find you. And the girl will be returned to her father – dead! For I ask the Spirits to ensure you both perish, so that all I have to carry back are your remains.'

Blue Bird shuddered and looked up at the grey sky with sombre clouds, asking the Spirits to deliver them safely from Zuni's wrath.

They paused when they saw vultures swooping over Tall Tree's body.

'It is the end of Tall Tree,' said Wild Horse. 'The order of life means his flesh can be taken so that other creatures might live.'

'It is not the end of Tall Tree,' said Blue Bird. 'His soul lives on.'

'How can the soul live on? Where would it go?'

'To the Spirits, of course. Where else would the soul go?'

'I don't know. I'm not even sure what a soul is, or that we all have one.'

'Why do you ask such questions, Wild Horse? The elders teach us that we all have a soul, that the Spirits look after it once our body has finished with it.'

'Even Zuni's?'

Blue Bird hesitated, not wanting to offend the Spirits. 'Even Zuni's,' she said. 'When his time comes.'

CHAPTER EIGHTEEN

WILD HORSE

Wild Horse walked fast, trying to block out Zuni's last words; words which clung to him like a snake to its kill, and made him wish that he'd been able to look on the bound hunter as a trapped wolf, not his own kin.

Should he have killed Zuni? His tread quickened to bury the grubs of doubt burrowing through his head. He turned away from where Tall Tree lay on the opposite riverbank, towards the Land of Hills. They must get as far away as possible.

'It's rugged,' he said, 'but we'll find caves to shelter in. The rocky hills are lined with river valleys and deep canyons.'

Blue Bird kept looking over her shoulder at Zuni.

'Tell me about the sabretooth and the cubs,' he said to distract them both.

But as she told him about finding the big cat in her cave, he only half listened. Questions jostled for answers. *How long does she think she can look after the sabretooth cub? Why am I helping this girl who is not of my tribe? Am I helping her, or am I hindering her by leading Zuni to her? What if Zuni does come after us? Will my actions make Bear Face proud?*

He knew the answer to the last question; so far he'd only brought further shame on himself. Maybe Zuni was right and he'd never be the man his brother was. Maybe he should run back and kill Zuni . . .

'You showed great courage, Wild Horse.' Blue Bird's voice filtered through his thoughts.

'What do you mean?'

'By turning your back on Zuni.'

'Some might see that as cowardly.'

'It would be easy to turn back and gouge the life out of him. I could see in your eyes you wanted to do to him what you stopped me from doing. But you'd have your cousin's blood on your hands. I think that blood would do you great harm.'

Wild Horse looked at Blue Bird, wondering how she had seen his thoughts.

She smiled. 'You were right. We must be strong and ignore his threats, let the Spirits decide his fate. If they allow him to live he can return to the tribe and gain some honour and even sympathy, by accusing us of nearly killing him.'

'He would do that,' said Wild Horse. 'Let's hope the Spirits decide wisely and allow him to die. Now we must hurry.'

The ground was very rocky and uneven, dotted with scrubbed grassland and cacti, so they made slow progress, even slower because they had to stop for Paska to feed the cub. Wild Horse tried to hide his frustration as he listened to Blue Bird's chatter, but she grew quiet as the night wrapped itself around them and they made camp by some trees.

Two sunrises later and they were deep in the Land of Hills. A wind set upon them, scratching their faces with its icy fingers and it was difficult to talk. Wild Horse was grateful for the peace, but it was as if Zuni's last words were echoing through the sound of the bitter wind scurrying to meet them.

They walked all day, heads down against the blustering barrage. No animal crossed their path and as darkness slid towards them again Wild Horse was eager to find somewhere to rest for the night. The cub started crying and Blue Bird crouched down with the two animals.

'Why must you groan each time we stop for Paska to feed the cub?' she spat at him.

'I don't groan.'

'Yes, you do. I know the cub slows us down, but it has a right to live. If you do not agree, then you should leave us now.'

'It's getting dark,' said Wild Horse. 'We should keep moving until we find shelter.'

'Well, you carry on and find shelter. We'll catch you up.'

'No, it's better if we stay together.' He squatted beside Blue Bird to help shield the animals from the wind. The sky had gradually turned from pale ice blue to dark grey, and any warmth was drained away, forcing bleakness over the lonely hills.

Blue Bird shivered. 'That sky brings snow.'

'You are right,' said Wild Horse. He had noticed it, didn't know why he was irritated that Blue Bird saw it too. 'We must hurry towards those high crags in the distance. They should offer us protection.'

They started running. As they drew closer Wild Horse saw the wide canyon they approached was scattered with a few trees on their side, and woodland the other side of the broad riverbed. Dead branches pointed to the darkening sky and low bushes hugged the top of a craggy ridge which dropped down beside them to the canyon.

They unloaded the packs from their backs, panting for breath.

Wild Horse said, 'You gather wood for a fire and I'll look for shelter and food.'

'Or *I* can look for shelter and hunt while *you* gather wood,' said Blue Bird.

'No.' Wild Horse began to run. 'I'll be quicker.'

'It would be good if you could find us a snake,' Blue Bird called out. 'All that's left of the sabretooth leg is the marrowbone for Paska to chew out.'

Wild Horse hoped to find something better than a snake. It was good to be alone, looking for somewhere to shelter from the brewing snowstorm, and the cold stone clutched his fingers as he clambered over the crags, eager to find a cave. Finding no cover, and no sign of any prey, he climbed to the top of the ridge, could see trees on the far side of the canyon – it might be easier to find somewhere safe there, but they would get too wet and cold walking there. As he dropped down to a narrow ledge large flakes of snow started to cover it, but he found a gap between two rocks, where one jutted over the other.

Wild Horse squeezed through the opening. It was only just tall enough to stand in at the centre, but it was dry and widened out so that they could all fit into it. *Time to hunt*, he thought, but as he emerged from the overhang he saw how heavy the snow was falling; he must hurry back to Blue Bird even though he hadn't yet made a kill.

The snow was tumbling down so fast that he could hardly see the place where he'd left her. She was jumping up and down and waving one arm at him, the other clutching the sling with the cub tight against her chest.

'What took you so long?' She hurried him to put on his pack and filled his arms with the biggest branches, as if daring him to complain about the heaviness, before she scooped up an armful. 'I hope the wait is worth it,' she said as she followed him, 'and not too far away. I don't want all this wood that *I've* gathered to get wet.'

Wild Horse didn't reply. He put his head down as he trudged over the rocks, weighed down with the firewood.

The snow had already covered his tracks to the shelter.

'I can't see anything,' said Blue Bird.

She was right. Everything looked different masked by the whiteness and Wild Horse was beginning to worry that he wouldn't find the gap when he recognized the ledge.

'Paska. Come back!'

Blue Bird called as the dog ran off, nose to the ground. 'Paska!'

'She'll be fine,' Wild Horse said. 'Come on. The shelter is up there.'

'She's picked up a scent. I could make a kill if I go after her.'

'You can't. The snow is coming down too heavily. As you said, we need to get this firewood into the shelter before it gets any wetter, and light a fire. Paska will be back.'

Wild Horse pushed his armful of branches on to the ledge, climbed up. Blue Bird did the same, calling Paska again as she pulled herself up to the ledge.

'She'll expect me to follow her. I'm sure she'll lead me to a kill.'

'When she sees you aren't behind her she'll come back.'

'What if she loses our scent in the snow? She won't know we've climbed up to this ledge.'

'She'll come back for the cub,' he said to reassure Blue Bird, though he wasn't sure he believed it.

Inside the shelter, as they rubbed fire-stones over the dry twigs, Wild Horse realised that if Paska didn't find them then the cub would die.

And though very small, it would be a morsel of meat.

CHAPTER NINETEEN

BLUE BIRD

B lue Bird wanted to believe that Paska would return, as she always did, but how would the dog find them up on this ledge with their tracks covered by the snow? It pained her that Wild Horse did not share her concern.

'I'm going to call for Paska. You look out for the cub.' She swaddled the cub in the sling and laid it near Wild Horse. He looked at her but didn't reply as Blue Bird stood by the opening to their shelter and shouted, 'Paska,' again and again. The thick layer of snow muted her calls.

She stayed there, watching and hoping, calling out from time to time. Resentment chewed inside her – Wild

Horse had expected her to collect the firewood while he searched for shelter and food. It had been more of an order than a request; too much like Mogoll. She was going to have to say something to him.

There was some satisfaction that he hadn't made a kill, while she'd collected plenty of wood. So much that they couldn't carry it all. They might be hungry, but at least they wouldn't be cold. Blue Bird still had some pemmican, a handful of nuts and a little dried fruit, but she hadn't told Wild Horse about that. Maybe she'd wait and see what food he'd brought. They'd have to eke out their supplies.

The cub's cry signalled it was hungry. She sat cross-legged by the fire and lifted it into her lap, dripping a little water on to her finger for it to suck.

'Come, Paska, your baby needs you,' Blue Bird whispered into the flames.

'Spirits alive,' Wild Horse cried out as Paska lurched towards him and dropped a fox at his feet, before shaking herself, covering Wild Horse in icy beads. 'Cursed animal!'

Blue Bird laughed as Wild Horse stood up to shake off the droplets while Paska snatched the cub from her lap and settled down to feed it.

'Well done, Paska,' she said, picking up the fox, though the rancid tang told her it wasn't a fresh kill.

'Huh,' said Wild Horse, 'it's obviously some other creature's kill.'

'Tell me, Wild Horse,' Blue Bird said, 'what food do you

bring that allows you to reject what Paska has found?'

She watched Wild Horse struggle to answer. 'I spent too long talking to your aunt, didn't have time to think about food.'

'I also talked to Sacred Cloud before I left, but I was wise enough to bring a few things from our store.'

'And do you have any left?'

'I have a little, which I am saving for when I am *very* hungry. I will share it with you, but only if you agree not to snort each time I offer some of our meat to Paska.'

'What?' said Wild Horse.

'You snort like an angry colt whenever I feed Paska. Maybe you think she belongs with a pack of dogs, just like Burning Fire did.'

Wild Horse hunched his shoulders.

'Paska has as much right to eat as us, especially as she's brought us food.' Blue Bird shook the fox under his nose. 'So you can either eat fox with Paska and me, or,' she offered him a twig, 'chew on some firewood. You're allowed to laugh,' she added, nudging his shoulder.

Wild Horse took the twig and pretended to take a bite, managing half a smile as he said, 'Fox sounds good to me.'

'And no more snorting?'

'No more snorting.'

'Good. Let's get this thing cooked before the smell gets any worse.'

Wild Horse laughed and Blue Bird grinned. She hadn't heard him laugh before and she liked it – it suited his face.

*

The snow eased off as they settled down to sleep, but was falling heavily when they awoke. The same thing happened the next day. Layer upon layer of white encased the canyon. They were wrapped in a cocoon and there was no chance to go hunting. Blue Bird rationed the meat from the fox, and added mouthfuls of pemmican now and again.

'This is good,' said Wild Horse, who hadn't eaten it before.

'I'll show you how to make it,' said Blue Bird, 'but not until there are ripe berries to pick. They have to be dried and pounded into dried meat. Sacred Cloud taught me; she said it was a favourite way of preserving food for the Snow Moons, that she'd learnt it from her mother.'

'The Snow Moons,' sighed Wild Horse. 'We've walked into them as they head back to the mountains beyond.'

'At least we have shelter,' said Blue Bird, determined to keep Wild Horse in a good mood.

Trapped inside, she talked about hunting, how Mogoll had taught her to hold a spear, and Wild Horse ignored her questions about his family, but told her how he'd taught himself to recognise animals by their tracks, their calls, their dung.

He showed Blue Bird the piece of chert his father had given him. 'It will make at least two good spear-points if I flake it carefully.'

She watched him break off two large flakes with his hammer-stone and start chipping them into points. As she played with the cub, Wild Horse made a shallow groove in each point with a fine tool made from an antler. It meant the point could be attached more easily to a fore-shaft or a spear.

By the third night they'd eaten all the fox and run out of firewood. The clear sky summoned another cold night. Blue Bird snuggled into the folds of her bearskin, curling around Paska for extra warmth, the cub safely nestled next to its new mother. She glanced at Wild Horse, just visible in the dying embers of the fire, and nearly suggested that he come closer to share their warmth, but decided he'd most likely turn down her offer. He wouldn't want to get that close to Paska. *Let the silly man-boy stay cold on his own*, she thought.

Brightness shone through the overhang when they woke the next morning, announcing that the sky was no longer heavy with snow. The fire had died in the night, and they shivered as they each had a mouthful of pemmican. Paska chewed on the bones.

'We must make a kill today, and get more firewood,' said Wild Horse. 'It won't be easy, but while I go hunting you can find the place where you left the rest of the wood that you gathered, and bring it back here to dry.'

Blue Bird said, 'I think we should stay together – collect the firewood and then go hunting.'

'No. It will be better if one of us does the hunting and the other watches over the fire.' Wild Horse shook his head. 'I wish I'd saved some dry kindling to restart it.'

'But you didn't.' Blue Bird smiled smugly. 'And as the person who brought the pemmican I also remembered to save some kindling.' She showed him the twigs she'd tucked out of the way, silently thanking Mogoll – he had taught his daughter well how to survive, and he would be proud of her, even though she was a girl.

A girl who had told Wild Horse about the hunting she had done, to show him she wasn't like the girls in his tribe. But he'd still given her the job of collecting firewood. She picked up her spears.

'What are you doing?' said Wild Horse.

'I'm going hunting with you.'

'It will be better if I go alone. It is what I am used to. I was brought up to be a hunter.'

'So was I until my brothers were born, and I managed to kill a snake and a rabbit before you arrived.'

'That was fine for you and Paska, but we need something bigger now,' said Wild Horse. 'I've told you how I've learnt to track and kill prey on my own. We need a fire to keep us from the cold as much as we need food. By saving the kindling you have shown your survival skills, so it is right that you are the one who sees to the fire.'

Before she could say anything else he was gone. Blue Bird brandished her spears at the disappearing man-boy, willing him to change his mind and come back. But he didn't. She stamped the floor of the shelter, cursing loudly.

How could she prove to Wild Horse that she was a hunter too?

She settled Paska with the cub before she set off.

The sky was bright blue and the ground twinkled, as if many stars had shattered in the night. *Maybe that's what happens to old stars*, she thought. *As they die they fly down to the earth*. But not her mother's star. Her mother's star was still young and shone down on her.

Blue Bird left deep footprints as she walked, so she knew she'd find her way back to the shelter. The dead wood was hidden under drifts of snow, so it took her a long time just to gather one armful. Numbness gripped her fingers as she knocked each piece against rocks to shake off as much snow as possible. It was going to take more than one journey to gather enough wood – if Wild Horse had been with her it would have been so much easier.

There was no sign of Wild Horse as she collected the last pile of wood. Her arms ached and she was as damp and cold as the firewood, as she rubbed her fire-stones over the kindling she had saved. It sparked into life and she gradually added the driest wood, then laid the rest of the branches and twigs near the fire to help the wood dry out.

Blue Bird sat down by the fire and played with the cub to tire it out, throwing twigs for it to chase. She wondered how long it would be before they needed to wean it, how long before it became too big to carry in the sling. They'd have to hunt for enough meat to feed the cub as well as themselves and Paska. She knew that would displease Wild Horse.

When the cub finally settled down to sleep she picked up her spear. 'Come, Paska. Let's see what you can help me flush out of the undergrowth.'

And there it was. Nibbling at the remains of the greener

twigs Blue Bird had gathered but not bothered taking back for firewood.

A rabbit. It fell to the throw of her spear, Paska leaping forward to retrieve the body almost before it was on the ground. Blue Bird knew Wild Horse wouldn't be impressed, but at least she'd have something cooking by the time he returned and the rabbit was quickly gutted, skinned and set over the fire. She was surprised Wild Horse wasn't already back, since the moon would be rising soon.

She remembered last night's moon, full and round, and wondered how many moons it would take for her to find her mother's tribe. Sorting through the firewood, she chose a short straight branch and cut a thin section about the length of her hand and two fingers wide and smoothed it, using her scraper. If she carved a notch each full moon the stick would tell her how many moons they had travelled. She carved a notch with her flint burin, a sharp cutting tool, before putting the stick in her tool pouch.

Where was Wild Horse?

She cursed him for insisting on hunting alone. If only he knew how good Paska was at picking up a scent, and how well she threw a spear. He should be back by now. Maybe he'd failed to make the kill he'd been determined to bring back, and was too ashamed to return with nothing.

'You shouldn't have boasted about your hunting skills, son of Bear Face,' Blue Bird whispered. 'The Spirits don't like it.'

CHAPTER TWENTY

WILD HORSE

Wild Horse left the shelter carrying three spears, with spare points and a knife in his belt-pouch. That Blue Bird had been the one to save some kindling chafed him like stones rubbed into a sore. He had to return with a large kill.

He walked along the floor of the canyon. The deep drifts dragged his legs, like wading in a swamp. A rabbit scampered under snow-covered shrubs when it saw the hunter, but Wild Horse had his mind on bigger things. He decided to clamber up the high wall of the canyon to get a longer view.

His hands turned blunt with cold as he struggled

higher, and he lost his grip and slipped off a ledge. The snow provided a soft enough landing, but as he walked on his toes started to throb. The moccasin hide had been scraped and rubbed with animal fat to make his moccasins waterproof, but snow had burrowed inside when he fell. Wild Horse took off the moccasins to shake out the frozen lumps, but he was shivering and he hoped that Blue Bird had collected plenty of firewood.

The slippery ice made climbing treacherous, so he decided to go back down to the canyon floor, which was spanned by a river much wider than the river they'd left behind. Wild Horse could see jagged rocks jutting out of the frozen river, half hidden under their snowy shell. If the ice between them was thick enough to take his weight he could get across, using each rock as a place to check for thinner ice. Then he could head into the woodland, where the trees, wrapped in their white shroud, would offer better cover for animals.

But as he got closer he saw that the rocks were further apart than he'd hoped. He stepped on to the frozen river and leant forwards to test it. There was no movement – it should be safe enough.

Wild Horse trod carefully as he made his way from rock to rock. The ice creaked with each step, but didn't crack. He'd nearly reached the last rock when he saw a small herd of deer moving through the trees on the river-bank ahead. He hunched down slowly, careful not to be noticed. If he slid across to the next rock, once he had a firm footing he should be able to jump for the riverbank.

The deer would scatter, but he'd be ready to throw his first spear and chase them.

Before he had a chance to move the deer dashed away. He frowned then saw the reason.

A grey wolf, prowling out from the trees.

It glanced at the retreating herd, but turned towards the frozen river. Wild Horse watched the creature sniff the air, baring its yellowed teeth. It was not part of a pack, or it wouldn't have been hunting the deer on its own.

It was thin and hungry.

And coming towards him.

Wild Horse kept as still as possible, but the wolf came closer. It slithered down the riverbank, started to slink across the surface of the frozen water.

Wild Horse pictured Blue Bird waiting for him and knew he had to kill the wolf – he couldn't risk it crossing the river and following his scent back to where she was. He lurched forwards to throw his first spear – and as the spear flew the surface of the ice cracked, plunging him into the freezing water.

Its coldness bit into him – silencing the yell in his throat. But the wolf yowled; the spear had sliced through its ear and it was now angry as well as hungry.

Wild Horse lunged back at the rock, tried to haul himself out of the river with one hand as he clung to his remaining two spears with the other. His fingernails clawed at the slippery surface, but he couldn't get a good enough grip.

The wolf leapt at him, but crashed through the ice.

Again Wild Horse tried to clamber on to the rock, again he sank back into the freezing water. He was surrounded by huge chunks of broken ice, could no longer see the wolf, could feel numbness squeeze through his legs . . .

A sudden growl behind him and Wild Horse turned to see the wolf's head rise out of the smashed ice, eyes wild, jaws open, jagged teeth glistening. Wild Horse twisted his whole body round as he thrust at the wolf with both spears. The points gouged into the creature's shoulder, but it wasn't ready to die. It writhed, breaking more ice, and knocked Wild Horse below the surface. All he could do was grab at the wolf's rear legs.

Hunter and wolf grappled under water until both thrust their heads upwards, gasping for air. Wild Horse grasped for the knife in his pouch and stabbed it into the beast's neck.

The wolf's howl boomed across the frozen landscape.

Wild Horse clung to the rock and watched the wolf's body sink under the ice.

The air was suddenly still apart from Wild Horse's heaving breaths. Half expecting to see the wolf charging out of the water again, he thrust his knife back into the pouch and then pushed his exhausted, numb body towards the riverbank, huge chunks of cracked ice crashing against his chest. It seemed to take for ever. When he stumbled on a rock and slipped beneath the surface he was sure he didn't have the strength left to lift himself back up again, but with one last effort he pulled himself out of the river by clutching at the base of a low shrub, dragging his legs behind him.

He collapsed on to the frozen ground, his whole body shuddering, apart from his legs – which were surely attached to the rest of him, but lay there as rigid as felled tree trunks, as if they didn't belong to him. He rubbed his jaw to ease a stinging sensation, saw the blood on his hand where the wolf had clawed him. He knew that the scent of fresh blood would attract any passing predator, but he had only his knife and two points to defend himself from attack. No spears to throw, no legs to run with.

He looked up to the sky and asked Blue Bird's Spirits to look after her. She would be waiting for him, not knowing he could not return. At least the wolf could not harm her. But there were many other creatures out there. She was on her own, and so was he.

CHAPTER
TWENTY-ONE

BLUE BIRD

Blue Bird could wait no longer. Something bad had happened to Wild Horse. She had to find him.

His tracks were easy to follow, hollows in the deep snow. Blue Bird could see them stretching out before her, tried to step into them, but his strides were longer than hers. She bounced from hollow to hollow – it helped keep her warm. He'd gone a long way; the craggy crevice that concealed their shelter was left behind.

Even though the sun was dipping behind the hills, darkness would not be allowed to fall; it was under the shimmering spell of the snow. The full moon also cast its light over the pale landscape. Was he buried in the snow? It was a terrible thought.

Blue Bird found a depression and scrabbling marks that showed Wild Horse had fallen from the rocks above. There were tracks which she followed along the floor of the canyon: tracks which stopped at the edge of the frozen river. But imprints on the snowy ice showed that Wild Horse had crossed it, or at least tried to.

Blue Bird fell to her knees, her breath quickening and sending white puffs into the cold air. 'Please, Spirits, don't let him be drowned. Don't let him be frozen to death,' she whispered. 'Wild Horse,' she called out, not very loud at first, but then louder and louder. 'Wild Horse, can you hear me?' She waited for a sound, any sound, to tear through the hushed veil that hung in the air left empty by her cry.

Nothing. She started to cross the frozen river, following his tracks from rock to rock. When she got halfway across she could see the wide stretch of broken ice on the far side and she clutched at the rock, scraping her fingers but not feeling the pain.

'Wild Horse!' she screamed into the snowy silence, not knowing that she could scream that loud. She tried to blur the image that flashed into her mind, of Wild Horse dissolving into the ice.

'Wild Horse!'

'*Blue Bird . . . ?*'

A faint call. She couldn't believe it. All her nerves

jangled. She couldn't see anybody. *Had she imagined it?*
Had she wanted to hear that voice so much that it had bled
into her ears?

But she had to believe she had heard it.

'Wild Horse, where are you? I'm coming to you.'

'No, you mustn't.' A figure slowly pulled itself from
under some bushes. 'The water is deeper on this side and
the ice is thinner.'

'What happened?'

'There were deer. I was trying to cross. A wolf . . . the ice
cracked . . . I ended up in the water with the wolf.'

Blue Bird heard the rapid *click-clack* of his teeth, saw
how his body trembled. Why didn't he stand up?

'Where's the wolf now? Are you hurt?'

'The wolf is dead, but so are my legs. I see them, but I
do not feel them. *I can't walk*, Blue Bird.' Wild Horse
raised himself against a rock, but he fell to the ground as
he tried to stand. 'I can't get back across like this. You must
return to the shelter before night comes, and with it even
more cold. Leave me here.'

'I'm not leaving you,' said Blue Bird. 'You have strong
shoulders, son of Bear Face. Use them. Pull yourself along,
slither like a snake.'

'The ice will break.'

'Not if you spread your weight, if you slide along the
ground away from the cracks. It looks safe to cross up
there.' She pointed to a place only a short distance away
from him. 'You can't stay out here, Wild Horse. You'll
freeze to death. This is your only chance.'

He set off slowly, then stopped. 'It pains too much. Do as I say, and go back to the shelter.'

'I've had enough of doing as you say. I got the firewood. Now I'm coming to get you.' She moved to step off the rock.

'Stop,' murmured Wild Horse. 'Stay there. I'll come to you.'

Blue Bird watched him slip down the bank and slowly writhe across the frozen river. His contorted face showed Blue Bird the pain gnawing at him. She sprawled out on the rock, arms outstretched, muttering encouragement, her teeth chattering like his.

At last she clasped one of his hands and dragged him on to the rock. She didn't mention the dried blood scoring a line from the side of his chin down his neck as she curled her body round his to ease his shivers.

'Come on,' she said. 'We need to get back.'

Wild Horse groaned. 'Let me rest.' His eyes kept closing.

'It's not safe to rest here. We must get to the land.'

'I can't move any more. I must sleep.' He laid his head against Blue Bird.

She looked up to the sky. A star was flickering. 'You can move, Wild Horse,' she said. 'Do it for Tall Tree. His spirit is up there willing you to live. I see his star. He didn't die so that you should give up. You must keep going.'

Wild Horse opened his eyes. 'Where are you, Tall Tree?'

'See,' she pointed. 'There is Tall Tree. He is with you.'

Wild Horse jerked his head as if to wake himself, then he lurched forwards using his elbows.

Blue Bird looked up to the star and whispered, 'Thank you.'

When they reached land she pulled up his leggings and rubbed his legs gently. He screeched like a bird caught in a trap.

'Sorry, I need to get some life back into them.'

'You sound like my mother.'

'Then be a good boy and take the healing.'

'I'll take the healing as a hunter, not a boy.'

'If you're a hunter, why put yourself in such danger when you're on your own?'

'Hunters take risks.'

'And work together, to share the risks.'

'I had to go hunting, while you collected firewood.'

'We were in a place unknown to either of us, surrounded by bad weather. We should have collected firewood together and hunted together.'

Wild Horse said, 'But you're a girl.'

'Yes!' Blue Bird yelped. 'And as I've tried to tell you, I'm also a hunter.' She didn't give him time to speak. 'And if there is no big prey it is better to kill something small than have nothing to eat. I realise it's not worthy enough for you, but I've left a rabbit that I caught, cooking on the fire that I built, with the firewood I collected.'

It sounded more boastful than she had intended.

Wild Horse looked down, said nothing.

'And the meat will be dry and chewy by the time we get

back.' She rubbed his legs, harder, causing him to wince. 'You have bad frostbite. I once saw my aunt treat it. If you think your legs are painful now, it will be worse tomorrow. I'll wrap my legs round yours to bring some warmth to them. But we must set off soon.'

His body tensed as she curled around him, but Wild Horse was too weak to argue. Blue Bird saw how the snow-covered top of the canyon gleamed with frost under the clear night sky, felt the cold nip her fingers and ears. They couldn't stay exposed for long. She had to get Wild Horse back to the fire – to get proper warmth into his legs, or they might stay numb for ever.

Wild Horse leant on Blue Bird as they set off, stumbling a few steps before falling. The ground was freezing hard and slippery, making it even more difficult for him, so he slid along on his backside rather than try to walk. It was very late by the time they arrived at the shelter.

Blue Bird let Wild Horse keep his breechcloth, but insisted that he take off his wet moccasins, leggings and tunic, so that they could dry out by the fire. There were deep gashes round one of his ankles.

'You didn't say you'd been wounded there as well,' she said.

'My legs are so numb I didn't know. The wolf must have bitten me when we were under the water. What do you mean – *as well*?'

'This.' She pointed to his chin.

'I forgot about that.'

Blue Bird gently applied Sacred Cloud's balm to all the

wounds before wrapping the camel skin round Wild Horse's shivering body. He hugged it tightly around him as he ate, and sat close to the flames. They ate most of the rabbit, ignoring its dryness, leaving a little for the next sunrise. Blue Bird gave Paska some before she wrapped up the remains of the meat and put it at the back of the shelter.

'What are your thoughts, son of Bear Face?'

'The wolf, lost on the riverbed. To kill a beast and then not get a chance to eat it, such a waste.'

'There will be other creatures who feed on the carcass. Any remains will be delivered back to the land. It will not be wasted.'

'I know, but I hunger for such meat. And my spears. I lost my spears.'

'You hunters and your spears.' She grinned. 'Be glad I took Tall Tree's.'

'See, I was right. You don't count yourself as a hunter. You said "you hunters", as if I am a hunter, but you are not. What are you?'

'I am a girl who can hunt. I can also build fires, pick the best berries, dig up the finest roots, find the right leaf to ease a sore wound.'

'Is there anything you can't do?'

'I can't please my father because he wanted me to be a son. And I can't make my mother proud because she died when I was born.'

'I think Mogoll and your mother would both be proud of you if they knew you came looking for me. You were very brave.'

'Of course I came looking for you. What else would I do?'

'I thought you'd wait here where it's dry and safe. You left Paska and the cub, not knowing if you'd find me.'

Blue Bird shook her head. 'You still don't know me very well.'

Poor Wild Horse, she thought. *You also don't know what suffering lies ahead of you.*

She remembered helping Sacred Cloud with a young hunter whose foot had been trapped in a frozen water-hole. He had suffered much pain. Wild Horse had survived the wolf attack, but now there was the night to get through. The throbbing in his legs would grip him fiercely, and a fever would come and shake his whole body. She looked into the fire, watched the flames flicker, heard the twigs crackle and spit.

I'll build up the fire, make sure it lasts through the night,' she said. 'You must keep warm.'

When the fever did arrive, Wild Horse quivered, shaking off his camel skin, calling out with confusion as it took hold.

'Tall Tree,' he wailed. 'Where are you? Show me your star.'

'He's with you,' Blue Bird said as she fed him sips of water, dabbed his forehead with droplets. And she made sure the fire didn't die down. All night she tended to him, hardly getting any sleep. She moved Paska, already wrapped round the cub, behind Wild Horse, so that he had warmth from both front and back.

As morning light crept into the shelter Wild Horse fell into a deep sleep and was still at last. Blue Bird hoped the worst of the fever had passed but she knew that when he woke again he would be very weak and in pain – not that he'd admit it to her.

She played with the cub till it grew sleepy, then placed its curled-up body next to Wild Horse. They could keep each other warm while she and Paska hunted and collected more wood. It would take a few sunrises for Wild Horse to regain his strength, and they couldn't travel far with so much snow on the ground, so she had to find food for them all.

Outside, clouds chased each other across the blue sky and wisps of hair drifted across her face. It wasn't the icy blast of the past few days; a thaw was starting. Blue Bird praised the Spirits for chasing away the eagle-spirit that opened its wings to bring snow, then she began to look for any signs of prey. A crashing sound behind made her swirl round, ready to attack whatever it was, whoever it was.

Zuni?

But it was a chunk of melting snow falling off a ledge.

The sudden thought of Zuni shocked Blue Bird; he still lurked at the back of her mind. She shut her eyes to be rid of him and replaced him with a picture of her mother. She'd never seen her mother, but Sacred Cloud had described her so that Blue Bird could see her in her head, and her mother had a softer rounder face than her sister, with the same green-brown eyes as Blue Bird.

Sacred Cloud had told Blue Bird that her mother made the best pemmican, instinctively knowing what mix of meat and berries would taste the best, would store for the longest. She'd said that the land they travelled as children had the sweetest berries. It had different trees. There were more rivers and lakes, fewer mountains and hills. The tribes travelled shorter distances, and knew each other.

When Blue Bird had asked her aunt why they had never returned, Sacred Cloud said that Mogoll preferred to roam the edges of the Great Plains, with its surrounding forests and river canyons, where there were more bison and mammoth. But Sacred Cloud thought the real reason was that, having lost his wife in childbirth and with no surviving son, Mogoll must have felt that the Spirits were punishing him for taking his wife away from that place.

'Spirits, don't punish me for being the daughter of Mogoll,' Blue Bird whispered into the breeze. 'Please help me find the home my mother had to leave.'

CHAPTER
TWENTY-TWO

WILD HORSE

Wild Horse pulled on his leggings. The hide chafed his legs, sending sharp slivers of pain into his flesh. He tried not to grimace, didn't want Blue Bird to see his agony. It was wrong that she had been hunting alone while he had been sleeping. And she'd let him sleep until the sun was high in the sky. If he'd been with her they'd have been more likely to make a kill. She'd brought back firewood, but no meat.

'Do you know what our shaman used to tell us?' said Blue Bird.

'No.'

'He told us,' Blue Bird continued, 'that if you are brave and strong without also being wise, your life will not be a long one.'

Wild Horse grunted. He was trying to remember what had happened before he fell asleep.

'I have seen you being both brave and strong, Wild Horse. Now you have to be wise. You are too weak to hunt. You must rest by the fire to regain your strength.'

He stamped his foot like a trapped colt and a spasm blasted through his leg. Blue Bird was right. His legs throbbed with pain, and his body would suddenly shudder. He hobbled to the fire.

'Let me put more balm on your wounds,' said Blue Bird.

He agreed to remove his leggings and sit near the fire with his camel skin draped over him. Blotches the colour of the night sky were creeping across his legs; blisters emerging. He flinched as she dabbed. Even though her touch was gentle, it felt like she was piercing him with hot points.

They ate the meagre remains of the rabbit before Blue Bird went out again, hunting with Paska, leaving Wild Horse to take care of the cub. His stomach groaned at the thought of spending the night with hunger gnawing at him, but he doubted Blue Bird would come back with anything. If only he could join her . . . but he was too weak.

And he felt so tired. He wrapped his camel skin around him and lay down by the fire. The cub was curled up asleep, its mottled fur bristling gently in time with its breaths, its whiskers twitching occasionally.

It would be easy to slip his hands round its throat . . . He would make sure its death was quick. He imagined skinning the small body and laying it on the hot stones nestled in the fire. In his mind the flames spluttered as the juices ran down the stones.

He reached for his knife . . .

'Oh, little one.' Blue Bird's voice rang into his ears.

Wild Horse jerked his hand upwards. But he wasn't holding his knife. It had been just a bad dream.

Blue Bird threw something to the ground before lifting up the cub. 'Just as well we came back when we did. The fire's nearly died, and this little one has woken up while you've been sleeping.'

Wild Horse gazed into the faintly glowing embers. He shook his head to blot out his mind's image of bulging eyes as he squeezed the young sabretooth's throat.

'Are you all right?' she asked.

He didn't know what to say, tried to blink away the vision as Blue Bird put the cub to Paska's teats.

'What do you think of this?' He looked up in time to catch what Blue Bird picked up and threw at him. 'It's a piece of dung,' she said, gathering bits of wood to rekindle the fire. 'I don't know which animal. Paska tried to pick up the scent to follow.'

Wild Horse had never felt so glad to handle animal droppings.

Blue Bird knelt down beside him. 'The droppings were by the river, but we found no tracks, so the animal must be too light to leave imprints deep enough to survive the thaw.'

'Raccoon, I think,' said Wild Horse, sniffing the small lump. 'You wouldn't see it in daylight. They eat fish, and worms, insects, berries.'

'That is the fur my father wears. It is thick and keeps out the cold.'

'That's right. The creature that left this behind has likely been sheltering in a rock crevice like us. It will be looking for food now in the dusk. I'll put on my leggings and we'll go hunting.'

Wild Horse needed to focus on killing something other than the cub. A raccoon wasn't a large animal, but it would provide them with enough meat for several sunsets. He stood up and stumbled towards the back of the shelter, but his legs crumpled beneath him and he beat his fist on the hard stone, overcome with fatigue and frustration.

Blue Bird came over to him. 'You must let me to do the hunting until you are strong enough. Tell me the best way to track the raccoon, Wild Horse. I'll use your knowledge to find it and then I'll kill it.'

Wild Horse couldn't argue. His legs wouldn't let him. 'If you return to where you found the droppings it's possible that it left them as a mark,' he said. 'Was the river thawed at the edge?'

'Yes, I topped up my water-skin.'

'Good. The creature might try a little fishing, or maybe scratch away some snow to find insects buried in the ground. But you'll have to be very quiet. They can't see well, but they can hear a worm burrowing beneath them. You need to go now as darkness falls.'

'I won't let you down, Wild Horse. With your guidance I will find the raccoon. If we don't see it by the river I'll send Paska into every crevice in the cliffs to flush it out. And this time,' she added as she left, 'no falling asleep. Make sure you keep that fire going and look after the cub.'

Wild Horse hardly dared to look at the cub once Blue Bird had left. He sorted through the pouch that contained his tools, laid out the ones he'd need for butchering, and added wood to the fire, anything to stop himself falling asleep again.

CHAPTER TWENTY-THREE

BLUE BIRD

Blue Bird was determined to return with a kill; she wanted to impress Wild Horse. She ran back to where she'd found the dung, Paska by her side, and they hid behind some rocks to scan the canyon wall for any sign of movement. Then they waited.

Even though darkness was casting a murky gloom over everything, the distinctive flash of white fur above the dark eyes and round the muzzle made it easy to catch sight of the raccoon. As it emerged from a crevice Blue Bird recalled Wild Horse's words, that it couldn't see her. It was smaller than she'd hoped for, but bigger than a rabbit. It climbed slowly down the rocks, pausing at the foot of the cliff, its ears twitching and its nose in the air sniffing for any sign of danger.

Blue Bird kept hold of Paska to make sure neither of them made any noise. The raccoon suddenly stood up on its hind legs. Something had alerted it. Blue Bird gripped her spear, cursing whatever it was.

A coyote crept out of the shadows, its ears drawn back, the black-tipped guard hairs down its back bristling. Blue Bird felt her body shudder. The coyote was bigger than the dog, and she'd never hunted such a creature on her own. She glanced at Paska, who raised her nose and bared her teeth – she'd picked up the scent of the coyote.

The coyote did the same. It knew where Paska was.

Blue Bird's breath quickened. She tried to swallow her own panic, but her mouth was dry. Would the coyote attack the raccoon, or was the smell of dog more tempting? As these thoughts rushed through her head she knew she had to make the first move.

Now.

She jumped up from behind the rock, Paska by her side. The raccoon hurtled away and the coyote stiffened, ready to pounce, its pale sharp eyes fixed on Blue Bird. Paska darted to the side, barking, as if to lure the coyote away from Blue Bird and the coyote leapt at the dog, its high-pitched yowl tearing apart the gloom. Blue Bird threw her spear, straining every muscle in her body and the coyote yelped as it hit the ground, its shoulder pierced by the spear. It pulled itself up snarling, ready to pounce again at Paska.

Blue Bird gasped for air, her chest too tight to breathe. Trying not to shake, she threw a second spear. It plunged deeply into the creature's neck and the coyote fell again. Blue Bird dropped to her knees, relief washing through her as Paska ran towards her, tail wagging.

'You were right,' Blue Bird gasped as she lumbered into the shelter, dropping the dead coyote on the ground. 'The raccoon didn't hear us . . . but a coyote smelt us!'

'What?' said Wild Horse. 'What happened?'

Blue Bird quickly explained how she'd killed the coyote, how brave Paska had been.

'You were very lucky,' said Wild Horse. 'Coyotes often hunt in pairs.'

'It wasn't just luck. Paska drew the creature away so that I could throw my spear.'

'Then you were lucky to have Paska.' Wild Horse smiled. 'The coyote is a good size and there will be plenty of meat. I'll have to butcher it from the light of the fire. Can you put more wood on?'

Blue Bird threw branches on the fire, sending puffs of smoke into the shelter. She was hoping for more appreciation of her hunting skills from Wild Horse. But as she watched him at work she realised how difficult it must be for him to accept that he couldn't hunt too.

The snow melted quickly and was gone in a few days. Wild Horse was determined to build up his strength so he walked a little each day, with Blue Bird supporting him. Gradually he stumbled less and they agreed it was time to move on.

As they set off Wild Horse said, 'I recognise this place now that it's not cloaked in snow; my tribe passed this way once. This wide canyon leads to a ravine.'

'And it heads towards the rising sun,' said Blue Bird with relief. At last they were going in the right direction.

For two sunsets they kept walking, slowly because Wild Horse tripped on the uneven ground if he tried to walk fast. Blue Bird could sense his frustration, tried to tell him that he was getting stronger, and she shouted praise to Tall Tree's spirit on the day that Wild Horse spiked several fish, using one of the spears that she'd taken from the fallen hunter's resting place.

'He is with us, Wild Horse, with you.'

'What do you mean?'

'Tall Tree. When he decided it was his time to die, not yours, his spirit chose to stay with you, to watch over you. I feel his presence. Don't you?'

Wild Horse said nothing.

He was right about the ravine, a narrow river valley with sharp sides reaching up to the sky. But it turned away from the rising sun.

'The water is very deep here, and the rock face is sheer, so it's not safe to cross,' he said. 'We'll have to turn away from the rising sun and follow the ravine.'

Blue Bird gazed along the ravine, dark shadows from the overhanging rocks hovering over the swift-flowing water. She knew that the Great Plains lay beyond, that they were even more barren, and beyond that were vast forests which led to the Great River. Her mother's tribe lived on the other side. It seemed so far away. Would she ever get there?

'Are you sure there's nowhere to cross?' she asked. She didn't want to lose sight of the rising sun again.

'You know there isn't, but if we walk through this ravine we'll reach a point where we can cross the river. After that we'll find easier walking as we leave this Land of Hills and reach the grassland.'

'Will that lead us to the Great Plains?' Blue Bird felt a pang of excitement.

'Yes, but first we should pick up one of the bison trails which lead to Blackwater Lake. It's a large lake where we should find plenty of animals to hunt before we set off across the Great Plains. Then we will head towards the sunrise once more.'

Blue Bird stared into the distance. 'You're right, son of Bear Face. Come, let's not waste any more time.'

'I think it is time you stopped calling me that.'

'What?'

'Son of Bear Face.'

'Why? It is part of who you are.'

'It is part of my past.'

'You can't run away from your past,' she said.

'It is my choice. I wish to leave it behind. Like you. You are running away too.'

'But I bring my past with me,' said Blue Bird. She

stroked first Paska and then the cub, snuggled against her in the sling. 'My memories and my life so far are part of me and belong with me always,' she added softly.

CHAPTER TWENTY-FOUR

WILD HORSE

A few days later the ravine curled towards distant mountains which clung to the skyline. Wild Horse knew it was time to cross the river. They had to leave it, even though it supplied them with fresh water and one or two fish.

The river behind them, they walked over the grassland, a welcome change to the stony hills. Wild Horse looked out for the bison trails his father used to follow towards Blackwater Lake, but he saw none. Maybe he'd missed the tracks? Or mistaken where he was? He walked as fast as he could, his legs much stronger now with just the occasional twinge of pain reminding him of the wolf attack.

'We need to make a kill,' Blue Bird said. 'Paska's milk will dry up if she doesn't eat soon. And the cub will perish.'

Wild Horse thought that might be a good thing. The little sabretooth was becoming difficult to control, often running off when they stopped, so they had to chase after it. Blue Bird said it was learning to be independent but Wild Horse knew that left on its own it would soon be dead. It should have been allowed to die with its mother, as nature intended. Humans and dogs weren't meant to rear sabretooths.

He didn't share these thoughts with Blue Bird as she called out to the Spirits for guidance, but he wondered how hungry she would be before she might agree to kill the cub or Paska...

At last Wild Horse saw faint marks on the ground. 'The edge of a herd trail!' He ran ahead. 'This will lead us to the lake.'

'How long before we get there?' asked Blue Bird.

'One, or maybe two sunsets. I'm not sure – it's been at least one winter since my tribe came this way.'

Blue Bird said, 'The Spirits answered my call. I send them thanks.'

'And I thank my father for teaching me about bison trails,' said Wild Horse, which surprised him. Maybe Blue Bird was right – he shouldn't run away from his past.

Before dusk fell they found a wooded area where they could make camp. Wild Horse passed Blue Bird the cub; it was too heavy now to carry for long periods, so they took turns. He shrugged off his own pack and grabbed two spears.

'I'll get some firewood,' he said, and dashed through the trees before Blue Bird could reply.

He knew she'd be annoyed that he'd set off alone, but at least he hadn't asked her to collect the firewood, and he just wanted some time on his own.

He stumbled, a reminder of the numbness that still pressed into parts of his flesh. As he moved through the undergrowth he realised that Blue Bird's chatter blocked two ugly visions: his fingers wrapped round the cub's throat, and Zuni's knife at his own throat.

If Zuni had made it back to camp, he might just take Night Rain as his wife and be glad to forget them . . . But he knew that his cousin would never forgive them for what had happened. Zuni would work out that Wild Horse and Blue Bird would have to cross the Great Plains at some point. The plains were vast enough for them never to meet again, but . . .

It was this doubt that gnawed at Wild Horse, like Paska chewed at a bone. It was partly why he'd chosen the longer route via Blackwater Lake – the further away they got from Zuni before they set off across the Great Plains, the greater the distance between them. Though he wasn't sure how they'd get across, since his tribe had never ventured over the Great Plains from the lake. But that all meant there was less chance of seeing his cousin again.

Neither he nor Blue Bird had mentioned Zuni since

they'd set off.

As he gathered branches into a pile at the edge of a clearing, a mewing sound seeped through the chirping of birds in the trees. The cub strolled into the middle of the clearing, sat down and looked at Wild Horse.

Stupid animal, thought Wild Horse. Why had it followed him? He was about to shout at it when he heard a rustle of undergrowth and a short-faced bear moved out of the shadows.

It was not full-grown, but its head was already level with Wild Horse's shoulders. It hadn't seen him yet, was too busy eyeing up the tasty morsel sitting in front of it – the little cub.

Not since he'd learnt to hunt had a prey come to Wild Horse so readily. It was also the biggest animal he'd seen since the wolf, and this time he was determined not to lose it. Blue Bird had hunted well when she'd slain the coyote – not that he'd told her so – and now he wanted to show her that he could bring down a big kill on his own. He kept very still, absorbing every twitch of the bear as it readied to attack the cub.

It seemed too simple. If he waited for the bear to pounce on the cub, he could grab his spears and kill the bear as it tore into the young sabretooth. They'd have enough food for many days, and the rest of their journey would be quicker without the cub.

But . . .

Wild Horse knew that Blue Bird would blame him for the cub's death, even though he'd left it with her. He cursed. He'd have to think of something else, something that would lead to a successful kill and leave the cub unharmed. That would please Blue Bird.

But he had to be quick. The bear looked ready to attack.

He flung down the firewood noisily to startle both animals. He expected the cub to run off scared, with the bear after it, allowing him to grab his spears and hurl them at the bear. But the cub didn't run away from the noise; it darted straight at Wild Horse.

With the bear right behind it.

It happened so fast. The bear was nearly upon him, grunting and growling, eyes glinting, mouth slavering, claws ready. Wild Horse acted by instinct. As the bear reared up on its hind legs to attack he lunged forwards, plunging his spear-point deep into the animal's throat. It made a strangled yowl as it fell in front of him.

Wild Horse could barely breathe as he grasped what had nearly happened, and his head felt like it would burst open. If he'd been any slower it would be his body lying there.

He knelt down with his knife to make sure the bear was dead and the cub crouched behind him, snarling. It was too tame, he realised. It had come to him for protection – and had put both their lives in danger. He'd tried to warn Blue Bird this would happen. She treated it too much like she did the dog.

'What happened?' Blue Bird ran into the clearing with Paska. 'I didn't realise the cub was missing. Paska picked up its scent.'

The cub went straight to the dog and started suckling.

'Your stupid cub nearly got itself killed.' Then Wild Horse grinned. 'Though it ended up being good bait. We've more than enough to eat now.'

'Bait? You used the cub as bait! How could you?' Blue Bird leant down to stroke the cub's back. 'Supposing the bear had killed the cub before you killed the bear?'

'And suppose the bear had killed me! You don't know what happened.' Wild Horse felt indignant. The cub was unharmed, and he had a good kill.

'You just told me. You used a helpless cub to tempt the bear!' Blue Bird was not listening.

Wild Horse said no more, but the bear carcass was too heavy for him to carry alone, even if his legs were fully recovered. It pained him but he had to ask Blue Bird to help him drag the body back to the camp.

They said very little until they started eating.

'We need bigger kills now, if we're feeding four,' said Wild Horse.

Blue Bird sighed. 'You don't have to remind me you do not agree about keeping the cub.'

'All I'm saying is the young sabretooth will soon be as big as Paska and will need more food than we do. Its natural mother would have brought back kills, started to teach it how to stalk prey. We can't do that.'

Blue Bird looked away. He was right, but she didn't want to agree with him.

*

The next morning they agreed to stay at the camp until the following sunrise so that Wild Horse could butcher as much meat as they could carry. The day passed quietly; no friendly chatter. Wild Horse finished the butchering before stripping off the bark of a dry branch; he whittled it into two spear-shafts. Blue Bird used her scrapers to clean the inside of the bearskin. Once it was dried out they could use it for shelter.

They continued following the herd trail the next sunrise, still hardly talking. After setting up camp for the night, emptiness prowled between them. Blue Bird tossed bits of her meat to the cub.

'You really shouldn't do that,' said Wild Horse.

'If I want to share my food with the cub, then I will. I don't expect you to share yours. I know you think it's a waste of meat.'

'That's not what I meant.'

'I know what you meant. You were hoping to get rid of the cub by using it as bait to catch the bear.'

Blue Bird spat out the meat in her mouth and stood up. She threw the bone she was chewing into the fire; it spluttered and crackled. Paska looked up, as if she had been expecting Blue Bird to throw the bone to her, so Blue Bird threw another bone to the dog. The cub walked over and Blue Bird stroked its head and fed it some more of the cooked meat.

'It deserves to eat as well as us.'

'Not like that.' Wild Horse stood up.

'What do you mean?'

'It will never learn to survive in the wild if you carry on handling it like you do Paska.'

'It's too young to survive in the wild without its mother. It needs us until it gets older.'

'It needs us to treat it like a wild animal, not feed it from our hands. In fact, why are you feeding it cooked meat? It should be having it raw.'

'I'm just replacing its mother for now. She'd bring it food.'

'She'd bring it a small deer to chew at, not serve up tasty cooked scraps.'

'You're just cross at sharing your food, sharing something you've killed by using a helpless cub as bait.'

'You weren't there so you don't know what happened.'

'You told me it was good bait for the bear.'

'Yes, it was, but not because of me. It did that all by itself. It didn't even know that a bear was behind it when it sat down in the clearing. The bear would have killed it if I hadn't been there.' He lowered his voice. 'When I realised the bear hadn't seen me I knew that if I waited for the bear to attack the cub it would make an easy kill for me.'

'I knew it,' Blue Bird said.

'Well, you knew wrong,' Wild Horse shouted, angry that she thought so ill of him. 'I knew how upset you'd be if the cub's life ended like that, so I tried to give the cub a chance to escape out of the clearing, but it ran towards me. With the bear chasing it. If my spear hadn't found its target we'd have both been mauled to death.'

'Oh,' said Blue Bird.

CHAPTER
TWENTY-FIVE

BLUE BIRD

B lue Bird was cross with herself. Wild Horse was right. She was treating the cub more like a puppy than a sabretooth cat that needed to be returned to the wild. And the more Wild Horse had disapproved of keeping the cub, the more she had petted it. If she continued protecting it like a tame animal the less likely it would be able to survive without her, without Paska. It was time to prepare it for a life without them.

From the next sunrise, Blue Bird started to train the cub. She let it walk for longer periods and tried not to panic if it wandered too far away from them. She could trust Paska to pick up its scent and bring it back. When they stopped to eat, she attached a chunk of the raw bear meat to a long piece of sinew, then hid in some bushes, throwing out the meat and jerking it towards her each time the cub pounced, just keeping it out of reach until she thought the cub deserved the reward.

Wild Horse laughed as the cub scampered off with its 'kill', the sinew trailing behind it. Blue Bird was relieved; Wild Horse seemed pleased with what she was doing. He hadn't said much since the bear kill.

They reached Blackwater Lake two sunrises later. The deep water glistened darkly, allowing the sun to shed a shimmering glow over the surface, rippled by paddling birds. Clusters of trees and bushes guarded its surrounds, all coming into leaf. High mountains loomed on the far side.

'It's beautiful!' said Blue Bird, breathing in the scent of the trees as she cast her eyes across to the mountains. 'I wonder if those are the Mogollon Mountains, where my father gets his name.'

Wild Horse shook his head. 'I don't know, but I have heard of them.'

Blue Bird ran to drink the cold clear water. They had drunk little that day as their water-skins were nearly empty. Paska and the cub joined her, lapping noisily.

Wild Horse said, 'It's a good waterhole for many animals, as well as humans. We should make a kill. The mammoths have probably already passed here, ahead of that late snowfall, on their way to the Great Plains. But there should be deer and horses, or bison.'

They made camp close to the lake. A small herd of white-tailed deer tiptoed towards the water and Wild Horse crouched down with his spears – just as the cub rushed past him.

The deer scattered like leaves in a breeze, the white underside of their tails raised in alarm, and Wild Horse jumped up and cursed the sabretooth as it chased after the frightened herd.

Blue Bird cursed it as well. Such bad timing. Just when Wild Horse was going to make a kill. But she didn't say anything, as part of her was proud of the little cub; it was responding to the training, had sensed it was a good time to attack. But another part of her worried that if it followed the deer too far it might get lost and be attacked by some other predator.

'If this place is as good as you say it is there will be more chances tomorrow,' she said, not admitting her concern about the cub, 'and we still have bear meat. Come, let's eat.'

As Wild Horse sat down beside her Blue Bird noticed that Paska had disappeared too, and she hoped that Paska would pick up the cub's scent and bring it back.

Darkness was descending when they returned.

Blue Bird woke to the songs of birds in the trees. Wild Horse was walking back from the lake, a smile creasing the corners of his mouth.

'Look what I caught.' He held up his spear to show two turtles pierced by the point. 'Thought it would make a change from bear.' He placed them over the fire shell-side down.

'The bearskin still smells strongly of bear although I scraped off as much flesh as possible,' she said. 'If we stay here a few days and stretch it out over a rock the warm breeze will dry it properly and lessen the odour.'

'You're right. It's no good if it attracts predators in the night,' said Wild Horse. 'The pelt will give us extra cover to shelter under. We'll find little protection on the Great Plains.'

Blue Bird said, 'It is a fine pelt from a good kill, a brave kill.' She was glad she'd offered praise to Wild Horse for the bear kill, even though she'd received none for killing the coyote.

There'd be fewer chances to find prey on the vast barren land of the Great Plains, so they needed a good store of meat.

A herd of bison approached the far side of the lake and started drinking – it would have made good hunting, but the beasts were too far for a spear to carry. They had to wait for something on their side. There were ducks and frogs and lizards which Blue Bird encouraged the cub to chase. But the cub always pounced too soon; it still didn't know how to stalk stealthily.

After one of these failed hunts, Wild Horse suddenly grabbed the cub by the scruff of its neck and crouched down beside it – Blue Bird laughed: they looked so funny together. Using his elbows, Wild Horse crawled towards a small snake winding through the long grass, holding the cub in one hand, his knife in the other. Just as the snake looked up he released the cub. It sprang ahead and landed with one claw on the snake's tail. As the head darted round, hissing, Wild Horse lurched forward and sliced through the snake's neck with his knife.

Blue Bird was grateful to Wild Horse for making sure that the cub's first catch didn't bite back; it might have been venomous. The cub ran around with the snake dangling from its mouth to show off its kill, before settling down to eat, growling at Paska that it didn't want to share.

'Here.' Wild Horse tossed a chunk of bear meat to the dog.

Blue Bird looked away to hide her surprise. First Wild Horse had helped the cub and now he had done something for Paska. Normally he only showed understanding of wild animals. She liked this side of him.

The next morning they sat opposite each other, Wild Horse punching holes round the edge of the bearskin with his awl, as Blue Bird cut thin strips of sinew to thread through the holes. The cub was fast asleep, exhausted from its training.

Wild Horse suddenly ducked his head and silently put down the awl. 'A herd of pronghorn at the lake,' he whispered.

They were working behind bushes, hidden from view, and a breeze sweeping across the lake was blowing their scent away from the approaching animals. Wild Horse reached for his spears and melted into the cover of the trees behind him.

Paska looked up as Blue Bird crawled to get her spears, but a silent command to stay was all that the dog needed. As she turned to follow Wild Horse through the trees Blue Bird could see the pronghorn drinking at the edge of the lake. She understood that Wild Horse wasn't expecting her to hunt with him, but she was Blue Bird, daughter of Mogoll.

She knew how to be as silent as a shadow, and she asked the Spirits to make sure Wild Horse didn't glance over his shoulder. Even though his stride was longer, she matched it, found the rhythm of his step, so that her footfall fitted his.

Her instincts were the same as his. She knew how quickly a pronghorn could turn and dart away with a point in its side before a second spear could be readied. She knew which animal was most vulnerable to attack. She raised her spear arm as Wild Horse raised his, kept her gaze steady on their prey, saw the animal twitch, knew it was time.

Blue Bird threw her spear at the same instant that Wild Horse threw his. The two spears found their target. As the pronghorn fell, Wild Horse spun round and his gaze met Blue Bird's, his eyes wide with shock, as if the Spirits had crept up on him.

Blue Bird didn't dare say anything, tried to stifle her gasp of delight, so unlike the breathlessness that had gripped her after the coyote kill, and she was grateful for the sound of hooves as the rest of the herd raced away. Wild Horse jumped up and ran with his knife to make sure their quarry was dead. Blue Bird decided it would be best to leave him and go back to the camp. She thought he looked annoyed, rather than pleased, that she'd helped with the kill.

'Stupid man-boy,' she muttered to herself as she thanked the Spirits for guiding her spear. Should she say sorry for sneaking up on him, for throwing her spear? Why should she? It was what her training had been for.

She watched Wild Horse return with the pronghorn stretched over his shoulders and she hoped his eyes would reveal what he was feeling, but Wild Horse looked down as he dropped the beast to the ground.

The thud woke the cub. It stretched and yawned, revealing the fangs that were starting to grow. Slowly it edged towards the fresh kill, nostrils twitching.

'You can wait your turn,' said Wild Horse, but the cub wasn't to be put off. Wild Horse grabbed his tools and quickly removed the lower part of a hind-leg. 'Here,' he waved it under the sabretooth's nose, then ran a little way with the cub in pursuit. He hurled the leg into the trees and the cub rushed after it.

'I didn't mean to startle you,' Blue Bird said as Wild Horse slashed open the underside of the carcass to remove the guts. 'It was my training with Mogoll,' she went on.

Wild Horse just nodded, the only sound that of skin being wrenched from flesh.

'Mogoll always said that if two hunters work well together, they stand a better chance of a kill.'

Still just a nod from Wild Horse.

'I knew how important it was to make a kill. We need meat for our journey across the Great Plains. That's why I followed you.'

Blue Bird sat down. She had said too much. Best to let Wild Horse concentrate on skinning the pronghorn. She started threading the sinew through the holes round the edge of the bearskin – it would hold it in place if they found a tree to shelter under. The pronghorn would make a fine pelt too; she would scrape off the fat and flesh and it could be made into pouches to carry spare points. The pronged antlers would make tools to aid the scraping.

'You threw well.' Wild Horse's words cracked open the hush that had enclosed them like a shell round a nut.

Blue Bird looked up, surprised. 'The Spirits guided my spear to follow the path of yours. I will praise them when we feast tonight.'

'It is Mogoll you should praise. He trained you well, though I think he knew you were a natural hunter. A hunter with skills that would make any father proud. And the coyote,' he added. 'That was a good kill. You are a true hunter, Blue Bird, and it will be an honour to hunt with you by my side.'

Blue Bird mumbled a 'thank you', unprepared for the praise that Wild Horse had at last granted her.

CHAPTER TWENTY-SIX

WILD HORSE

As he had approached the pronghorn Wild Horse had a strange sensation that he wasn't alone, that Blue Bird was right and Tall Tree's spirit was with him. When a spear flew over his shoulder, as he threw his, it was as if Tall Tree wasn't dead after all.

He had been stunned to turn round and see Blue Bird.

Now he watched her as he cut up the carcass. It was strange for her to be quiet; it was usually him. He had spoken the truth. She had thrown the spear very well. He must start thinking of her as a hunter, as a brother, not just as a girl who had run away.

This thought stayed with him when he went to sleep.

That was when Zuni arrived with many hunters. Too many against just the two of them. Wild Horse fought like a wolf, as he and Paska tried to protect Blue Bird . . .

Wild Horse awoke suddenly, gasping, and cursing that Zuni should lurch into his dreams so violently. He checked that Blue Bird and Paska were both all right before allowing sleep to return . . .

But Zuni's spear flew through the air, making sure Paska would never trouble him again. He tied Wild Horse's hands behind his back, threatened to slit his throat. Blue Bird screamed and scratched as Zuni dragged her away. Wild Horse wriggled and writhed to free himself of his bonds, wailed as Zuni and Blue Bird disappeared . . .

'Wild Horse?'

He jerked awake.

Blue Bird stood over him. 'I think you were having a nightmare. You howled like a dying wolf.'

Wild Horse tried to shake out the horror that lurked in his head. It had seemed so real.

'What troubles you, son of . . .' Blue Bird paused. 'Is there something wrong?'

'No,' said Wild Horse. 'Why would you think so?'

'The fear in your eyes. It lingers, even though the dream has passed. Tell me, Wild Horse. Tell me what brings such terror to you. It will help you release it.' She put her hand over his and the gentle warmth seemed to soften his torment.

'I don't know if it was just a dream,' he said. 'I wonder if it was a warning.'

'What do you mean?'

'I have lost faith in the Spirits since they took Running Bear and Tall Tree from me. But sometimes I have bad dreams. I wonder if it is the Spirits' way of sending me a sign of something bad that might happen.'

Blue Bird said, 'If you doubt the Spirits while you're awake, they can come to you while you're asleep. Sacred Cloud said that dreams can reveal our deepest thoughts, our hopes and fears. What happened in your dream?'

'I can't help feeling that Zuni will not forgive us for leaving him as we did, that he will come after us. That's what happened in the dream, the nightmare. He took you away.'

'Why have you not told me this before?' she asked.

'I didn't want to alarm you. And I felt guilty.'

'Why guilty?'

'Because I led Zuni to you and because I let him live. I wish I hadn't.'

'You didn't know he was following you. And we left him alive so that the Spirits could decide if he lived or died. If Zuni does live I'm sure that Mogoll and Night Rain will make sure he forgets about us. It is time to put him out of your mind.'

Wild Horse tried to be reassured by Blue Bird's words. 'There is still a risk of crossing Zuni's path, and he will have hunters with him.'

'And we will have each other,' said Blue Bird. 'I have

proved to you that I am worthy of carrying these spears.'

'Yes.'

'And you now accept me as a hunter?'

'Yes. I told you.' Wild Horse breathed deeply. 'We will hunt well together. The two of us.'

'Don't you mean four?' Blue Bird smiled, looking at Paska and the cub.

Wild Horse smiled too. It no longer seemed strange, not being part of a tribe. They had their own small band. 'You're right. The four of us, brave together.'

He looked up at the moon as it appeared between the scudding clouds. It seemed sliced in half in the sky, the other half shimmering in the blackness of the lake below. That was how it always was. It started as a sliver, gradually grew into its roundness, then slowly disappeared. But it always came back.

'If the stars truly are Spirits, do you think they guide the moon on its path across the sky?' he asked.

'I don't know,' said Blue Bird.

'And what about the clouds and the wind? Do the Spirits control them, or are they free to go where they want?'

'I think the wind chases the clouds across the sky, but I suppose the Spirits direct the wind.'

'But not the sun,' said Wild Horse. 'I don't think the Spirits have power over the sun. Unlike the moon it always rises and falls in the same place, day after day. I have learnt that the sun is the one true guide.'

'Maybe it is.' Blue Bird smiled. 'But what about those

days when the Spirits tell the wind to send the clouds, so that we can't see the sun? That shows that the Spirits have more power than the sun.'

Wild Horse nodded. He couldn't argue with that.

'I will ask the Spirits to send no wind or clouds tomorrow,' said Blue Bird, 'so that the rising sun is there to greet us when we set off over the Great Plains.'

And it was.

As they reached the last trees and bushes which fringed the lake they paused to look back at the shimmering black water, watched over by the massive mountains that clung to the skyline.

'Thank you, Wild Horse, for bringing me to Black-water Lake. I will remember it for ever as a good place, the place where you saw the hunter in me. But it is not our place to be. We must cross the Great Plains to find that.'

Wild Horse thought he'd remember it always too. As he turned towards the sunrise he wondered what wisdom would make them leave such a place of safety.

The lonely desolate prairie of the Great Plains stretched before them, and all around them, as far as the eye could see. Nothing but grass.

He'd never been here. His tribe had never crossed the plains this far from the Land of Hills. And now he knew why.

CHAPTER TWENTY-SEVEN

BLUE BIRD

'You have found us the Great Plains, Wild Horse, like you said you would,' Blue Bird said, trying not to despair at the view. 'The grassland will not last for ever.'

Blue Bird kept repeating these last words to herself as they walked, but there was no change in the land. Just grass. No trees. No birds. Nothing. The air was dry. No sounds of wildlife. No sign of life apart from the four of them. And the grass.

She found herself looking over her shoulder, checking

that the mountains were still there, but they were gradually disappearing. Wild Horse walked ahead of her, at a fast pace, saying very little.

'I suddenly yearn for canyons and rivers and hills,' she said, hoping it might bring out a reaction from Wild Horse, but he just kept walking.

By the time they started looking for somewhere to camp, the sun was setting behind them, casting its golden glow over the empty horizon. Even the tips of the mountains were no longer visible. There was no shelter to be found so they huddled together under the night sky.

Blue Bird said, 'The cub needs a name. I know it is a wild animal and we're only looking after it until it can survive on its own, but until then can we call it – *her* – something that she might come to, as Paska does?'

'You could call it Wild,' said Wild Horse. 'Maybe that will remind you what it's meant to be.'

Blue Bird was annoyed. 'I don't need reminding. The cub is responding well to the training. I just thought choosing a name might ease the boredom of the grass.' She poked him hard in the back with her finger.

'Ouch. What's that for?' Wild Horse turned towards her.

Blue Bird grinned. 'I thought I'd make you wild, seeing as you want the cub named after you.'

'That's not what I meant, and you know it,' he said, but she could hear the smile in his voice, and the moonlight caught a playful flicker in his eyes.

They awoke to a grey sky, a troubled sky, with no sign of

the sun. The still air stirred a little, not that there were any leaves to rustle in the whispering breeze.

'I think you forgot to remind your Spirits that we need the sun to set our course,' said Wild Horse. 'We don't even have the mountain ridge to look back on.'

'They're not just my Spirits and we know where we last had sight of the mountains.' Blue Bird pointed in the direction she thought was right. But it was dark by the time they'd settled to sleep, so she wasn't sure.

'Maybe . . .' said Wild Horse.

As they set off once more, Blue Bird asked the Spirits for guidance. There were no landmarks, just one or two shrubs in the distance and they were soon swallowed up by the endless grassland. And endless sky, which joined up with the land in every direction. Yet Blue Bird stayed hopeful that they were walking away from the mountains.

The dull dead sky pressed down on them all day as they trudged across the prairie, with no glimpse of the sun and no waterholes in sight. Blue Bird's hope was fading, but she wouldn't admit it to Wild Horse.

There was no change the next day – still no sun to guide them. They said little as they walked; words scratched their dry throats.

When they stopped by a cluster of low bushes clinging to the grassland Wild Horse said, 'I know everywhere looks the same, but I'm sure we've passed this way before.'

'I think you're right,' whispered Blue Bird. 'We're lost.'

She slid to the ground, shoulders hunched, Paska to

one side of her, the cub on the other. Wild Horse squatted beside her and she closed her eyes to blot out the realisation that they had walked so far, and yet were no further forward. She trickled a few drops of water on to the parched brown leaf that had become her tongue, and Wild Horse turned away as she dripped a little into Paska's mouth.

'It's my water, and Paska needs it as much as I do while she still suckles the cub.' Blue Bird scowled at him. 'If we're going to die lost and thirsty, a few drops of water given to Paska won't make that much difference.'

'No, you're right,' said Wild Horse, 'and we're not going to die.'

'Are you sure?' Blue Bird shivered. 'I feel such a chill suddenly.'

The warm dry air was swiftly turning cold and dark.

'Listen . . .' said Wild Horse, as a tangle of noises snarled the air.

'Look!' said Blue Bird.

A huge flock of birds swept towards them, chased by a blackening sky. Their screeching ruptured the air as they passed overhead, then faded as they sped off, replaced by a faint rumbling which in turn blared louder and louder, like the roar of a lion pack, fast approaching. Dust clouds blustered across the twisted grasses.

'A prairie storm,' hissed Wild Horse.

The wind whipped Blue Bird's hair across her face, dirt into her eyes. 'We are blessed by the Spirits that we stopped by these shrubs,' she croaked. 'They give us something to hang on to.'

'We must lie flat on the ground,' said Wild Horse, 'holding the trunk of the shrub with one hand and the bearskin over us with the other. It will give us protection.'

'What about Paska and the cub?' Blue Bird grabbed Paska with one hand.

'The animals can look after themselves. It is their instinct,' shouted Wild Horse. 'We must not let go of the hide, or the storm will steal it from us.'

Blue Bird frowned at Wild Horse as she pulled both animals close to her before taking hold of the shrub and the bearskin.

Then the day sky turned black and the wind wailed as it wound round them, twisted over the shrubs, like a coiling snake. Lightning slashed the darkness and a crack of thunder deafened Blue Bird, then another pressed itself through her whole body, made her shake with fear. She shut her eyes, tried to block it out.

A violent blue flash seared through her eyelids and Blue Bird opened her eyes to see a strange black tail twisting down from the storm clouds, whirling towards her.

'What's that?' she screamed above the din.

'It's a tornado,' yelled Wild Horse. 'But maybe a small one. Keep your head down. Hold fast.'

The wind ripped the bearskin from Blue Bird's grasp. She reached out to grab it, but the tornado wrenched it and her into its shrieking spinning cloud, sucking all the breath from her body.

She felt she was going to be ripped apart. She heard

Wild Horse wail her name and the cub howl, tried to cling on to these as her last sounds before going to meet the Spirits.

CHAPTER TWENTY-EIGHT

WILD HORSE

The tornado whirled away as suddenly as it had arrived, pursued by the snarling cub. Blue Bird's body lay sprawled across low cacti where the tornado had flung her like a scrap of hide. Wild Horse rushed towards her.

She must be broken, he thought. *We should have held on to each other rather than the bearskin.* The vision of her small body being wrenched away from him by the tornado crashed through his head. 'Blue Bird . . .' he whispered as he leant over her, and felt himself smile as she stirred and murmured something.

'I thought I'd lost you.'

'I thought I was lost.' She struggled to move, cried out in pain as the cactus thorns tore at her flesh.

'Keep still,' said Wild Horse. 'I'll lift you out.'

As gently as he could he took hold of Blue Bird and she clung round his neck as he pulled her out of the cactus. He felt her chest thump against his, and Paska jumped up and pressed her muzzle into them.

'What about the cub?' asked Blue Bird. 'The storm frightened her . . . I saw her run . . .'

Wild Horse laughed. 'You get caught up by a tornado and all you're worried about is the cub. But you're forgetting something.'

'What?'

'The four of us – brave together, remember? Look.' The cub was loping back towards them. 'It wasn't frightened of the storm,' he said. 'It was fearless and ran to save you when it saw you were in danger. And then it had to chase off the remains of the storm, after it dropped you.'

Blue Bird's face lit up.

'Can you walk?' he asked her as he placed her on the ground.

She said, 'Yes,' but he saw how the pain darted up her body.

The howling wind raced away, but the dark sky was suddenly filled with more clouds and rain began to lash down.

'Come, we must find some cover.' Wild Horse picked

her up again and carried her to the shelter of the shrubs.

There he wrapped her under the deerskin, making sure Paska and the cub were curled next to her for warmth. He burrowed next to her beneath the low branches of the shrubs, pulled his camel skin around him, and held his water-skin out to catch raindrops falling off the leaves.

They had water again. They had all survived the storm. And he hadn't lost Blue Bird.

'Thank you, Wild Horse,' Blue Bird said, 'for everything.'

'There's no need to thank me,' he said. 'I'm just glad that you live. I should have held on to you.'

'I shouldn't have reached out for the bearskin. It was my fault. I wouldn't have survived this storm if I'd been on my own.'

'And I wouldn't have survived a freezing night on the ice if I'd been on my own.'

'So we are the same.' She smiled at him.

'I suppose we are.' Then he added, 'But you were lucky. My father warned me about tornadoes. He once saw a huge rock twisted high into the air, which shattered into pieces when it hit the ground.' Blue Bird shuddered. 'But Bear Face's favourite tale was about the rabbit.'

'Oh no,' said Blue Bird, 'I don't want to hear what happened to the rabbit.'

He smiled. 'My father swears he saw a rabbit being lifted as if by gentle hands, carried through the air and softly placed back on the ground some distance away. The rabbit twitched its ears and ran off.'

Blue Bird laughed. 'I like that tale. I suppose the cactus saved me from a worse fall, though many thorns pierced me.'

'I'll pull those out when the rain stops,' said Wild Horse, 'but now I'm thinking you were right about the cub needing a name.'

'Really?'

'Yes. We should call her *Storm*. It – *she* – has earned it. She was brave as she chased it away from you.'

'Storm is a good name.' Blue Bird grinned. 'I hope she learns to come to the call of her name, like Paska does.'

'I'm sure she will.' Wild Horse grinned back. 'You've trained her well, Blue Bird. And it is time I helped with the training. She will grow into a strong beast. We must prepare her for her life in the wild.'

Blue Bird laughed. 'First you find the cub a name, then you say "she" instead of "it", and then that you'll help train her. I think the storm washed away your dislike of her.'

'It wasn't dislike – I just wanted to make sure she didn't become too tame. She has earned my respect. She deserves a chance.'

Rays of sunlight began drifting over the grassland, making it glisten. With the sun back to guide them they would not be lost.

Wild Horse helped Blue Bird pluck out the thorns from her arms and legs. She was bruised and scratched, could only walk slowly, but it didn't matter; at least she was alive.

They hadn't gone far when they saw the bearskin, draped over a rock.

'See, Wild Horse, I knew the Spirits would help us!' Blue Bird beamed at him. 'They saved the bearskin and left it drying for us to find.'

Wild Horse rolled it up and slung it over his shoulder. He didn't have Blue Bird's faith that all would turn out well. There were remnants of the storm in the endless grassland, puddles for the animals to drink from, but he knew they needed to find something better than puddles.

The watery sun was dipping down behind them when Wild Horse saw a short trail of dried brown lumps.

'Look,' he said. 'Camel droppings, and more over there. See how the dung beetles feed. The storm has revealed hoof marks too. A herd has crossed our path.' He turned to where the tracks led, with the setting sun to his side. 'They will lead us to water. We must leave our course and follow the trail.'

Blue Bird said, 'If the Spirits have sent us this guidance we must thank them and follow it.'

'It is the camels we should thank,' said Wild Horse. 'There are times when we follow the knowledge of the animals. Camels have roamed this land longer than we have. They travel long distances without needing to drink, getting moisture from the plants they eat, but there comes a time when they need water. Their hoof marks will take us to a waterhole, or maybe a lake or a stream.'

They set off, Wild Horse looking at the ground to make sure he didn't lose the trail. Light was fading when they at last saw trees ahead, a good sign. As they drew closer he heard the sound of rushing water. Laughing, he picked up Blue Bird and spun her round. Abandoning their packs, they scrambled through the trees and undergrowth down to a river.

It was the widest river Wild Horse had ever seen.

CHAPTER TWENTY-NINE

BLUE BIRD

Blue Bird gasped. 'Is this the Great River? The other side of the Great Plains.' She really wished it could be true.

Wild Horse shook his head. 'No, it can't be. But it's a powerful river which heads towards the rising sun, so I think it will lead us across the Great Plains.'

'And we have water,' said Blue Bird. 'I feel the Spirits are back with us. They tested us with the storm. Now they give us this . . . this big river! I'll call it the Big River.'

Wild Horse smiled. 'The Big River it is, and it will be

something else to look at other than the grassland. It's not a river my tribe has known.'

'That's good,' Blue Bird looked at him.

'Yes,' said Wild Horse. 'It means we are unlikely to see Zuni.'

Which was what Blue Bird wanted him to say.

The Big River took its time, snaking round rocks, rolling over falls and curling between trees. In spite of its winding course it continued to flow towards the rising sun. They kept it on one side as they walked, with the endless prairie clinging to their other side, reminding them of the bleakness they'd endured. It was a good time to be unhurried. Time to get used to hunting together, and to train Storm.

On the night of a full moon Blue Bird knew she must make a second notch in her stick. The moon lit the plains so brightly that they kept walking long into the night. A thin dark line appeared across the horizon ahead of them, and it had become thicker by the time they made camp.

Blue Bird soon realised what it was. 'Wild Horse. Look in the distance. It's the forest, as far as you can see.' She flung her arms round his neck. 'We've made it. The Great Plains will soon be behind us.'

And suddenly there was a need to hurry.

The next day, the sun was not yet at its highest point in the sky when they reached the forest. Trees stretched skywards all around them; leaves and pine-needles were scattered over the floor and feathery ferns danced at their feet.

Blue Bird stretched out her arms as she ran through the web of green, before letting herself fall on to the soft forest floor. She looked up into the tangle of branches and leaves. How strange it was, she thought, after so many days and nights of just sky above her. So different, so much to look at, smell, hear . . . The scent of pine-needles, the rustle of leaves, the chatter of birds . . .

'It is so long since I had something other than hard grassland to sleep on,' she said, jumping up. 'I have memories of collecting ferns with Sacred Cloud. Come, Wild Horse, fill your arms too. Help me gather something soft to lie on.'

'But it is too soon to make camp,' said Wild Horse.

'Oh, Wild Horse, won't it be good to lay your sleeping-hide over soft ferns?'

'Yes, but don't you see how far the forest stretches? If we continue our journey until the sun goes down there will still be ferns to collect.'

'But if we walk all day we'll be tired,' said Blue Bird. 'We'll have to collect wood for a fire, so we won't want to gather ferns. Let's stop here. There's got to be good hunting in the forest. We could do with some fresh meat.' She added, 'You don't have to collect the ferns. I'll do that. And I'll collect firewood. You make a kill on your own. Close your eyes and smell the cooking meat. Listen to the fire hissing and crackling as fat drips on to it. Taste those juices oozing out into your mouth . . .'

Wild Horse laughed. 'I give in. We'll camp here, but if I make a good kill on my own you might wish you were there.'

'I'll take the chance.' Blue Bird grinned. 'We've made it this far, Wild Horse. We've crossed the Great Plains. Soon we should come to the Great River. Once we cross that I'm sure we'll be close to my mother's tribe. Our journey will be done.'

Blue Bird ignored the strange look on Wild Horse's face as he set off; she was too busy gathering ferns to wonder why he looked suddenly sad.

It didn't take her long to collect enough for each of them to lie on, so she took one of her tools to dig into the ground in the hope of finding some roots to eat. Bugs marched around her, as if protesting about being disturbed, but there were no roots she recognised and she was soon beginning to wish she'd gone hunting with Wild Horse. She threw small branches and rocks for Storm to pounce on – the cub was responding well to their training.

After collecting firewood she built a big fire and it was soon roaring. Where was Wild Horse? She was surprised he hadn't returned and she thought about going to find him, but didn't want to spoil his chance of making a solo kill. She asked the Spirits to guide him.

Blue Bird spread the bearskin over the ferns and lay down, enjoying the softness, but her enjoyment was spoilt. It seemed wrong that she was doing nothing, while Wild Horse was hunting in the forest alone. What was taking him so long? What if something had happened to him? She shuddered as she remembered how she'd found him after the wolf attack on the frozen river. How stupid of her to suggest he went hunting on his own just because she wanted to gather some ferns. Especially as they'd learnt to hunt so well together.

She walked to the edge of the forest, Paska and Storm at her side, and tried to crush the seed of worry growing inside her.

CHAPTER THIRTY

WILD HORSE

Our journey will be done. Wild Horse ran into the forest with Blue Bird's words gnawing at him. What would he do when they found her family? Would he stay with them? He hadn't had a plan for his own journey when he had left his tribe, so he'd chosen to help Blue Bird. They'd survived many dangers together. Enough to stay together? Enough to make Bear Face proud? Wild Horse wasn't sure if making his father proud mattered to him any more.

He breathed in the smell of the trees, trying to clear his mind. The forest was dense; it would be easy to get lost. He scored a mark on the trunk of a large tree, as the hunters of his tribe had been taught to do, something to look out for on his return.

When he found a deer trail leading from a clearing, Wild Horse realised it seemed strange not having Blue Bird with him. She would have been as excited about the find as he was. He should have helped her gather ferns, and then they could have hunted together. As he considered going back to get her, a young hind jumped into the clearing and the decision was made for him: he'd stay. It was too good a kill to miss. Wild Horse took aim.

A sudden clatter of hooves in the distance sent the hind scuttling away. Wild Horse's point was in its side and the fore-shaft had broken away from the spear as it was meant to, but the point hadn't gone in deep enough to bring the animal down. Wild Horse grabbed the fallen spear-shaft and ran after the injured hind; he ran between trees, over hillocks, through huge ferns, managing to keep pace with it, hoping that the blood loss would slow it down or he'd get close enough to throw another spear.

When he tripped over a creeper the hind was lost, and so was he. He'd been so distracted by his thoughts of finishing the journey, as well as the thrill of the chase, that he hadn't scored any more trees.

It was so different from the stillness of the plains. Too many sounds. Birds shrieking and humming, a distant thumping of hooves, leaves rustling, the crackling of broken twigs . . . sounds which unnerved him because he'd grown so used to the silence of the plains. For a moment, he thought he heard the faint sound of a voice and he stood rigid. Then it was gone – it must have been inside his head.

When he reached what he thought was the deer trail again the forest noise started to fade behind a din that was getting louder and closer: a thudding on the ground and the loud cracking of splintering trees. What was it? A mastodon? The ground beneath him started to shake. He had to find cover.

He swirled round, wondering which way to run – he didn't have much time – and decided to go upwards. If he climbed the tallest tree he'd be able to see what was approaching. Making sure his spear-shafts were held tight in the bag on his back, and his points and knife were safe in the pouch tied to his belt, he scrambled up the wide trunk of a tree with good overhead foliage.

Perched on a branch near the top, hidden by leaves, he waited for the animal to appear, a spear held ready in case of attack. He couldn't believe his eyes when the creature lurched into view.

Not a mastodon but a giant sloth, as big as any bull mammoth he'd ever seen.

The claws on its front feet were the size of Wild Horse's arms and they reached out like curved knives, forcing it to walk on the sides of its feet.

It was eating young saplings, ripping them out of the ground as it did so. Wild Horse stayed very still. Would it catch his scent?

All of a sudden the sloth reared up on its massive hind legs, leaning back on its broad muscular tail. It was as tall as the trees, its head at the same level as Wild Horse's. The creature swung its claws to grab the choice young leaves from the top of the trees and Wild Horse feared he might topple out of the tree like a fledgling.

Just as he had decided he might be safer on the ground, the giant sloth turned and swiped at the branch he was sitting on, catching his jaw with its claw. He stifled a yell of pain and pressed his body against the trunk, his heart in his throat. He was about to slip down to a lower branch when he heard another sound.

A sound that grabbed his shoulders and shook him.

Cla-cla-cla.

The last time Wild Horse had heard that sound Tall Tree had died . . .

His fingers tightened round a branch as a band of hunters ripped through the undergrowth. The shriek of the huge sloth, as a spear caught its side, seemed to sum up the despair that pierced Wild Horse when he saw who had thrown the spear.

Zuni.

Wild Horse could only watch as more spears were thrown and the giant sloth reeled round and down on to all fours. Its massive curved claws slashed through one of the hunters, who fell to the ground with a haunting death cry.

Wild Horse scraped his fingernails on the bark as he slid down to a lower branch, on the far side of the trunk. The creature had ripped off most of the leaves there. Could the hunters see him? He didn't dare move, but he peered round the trunk, his breathing heavy at the shock of seeing his cousin. He couldn't take his eyes off Zuni.

The giant sloth rose to its back feet again, its solid limbs swiping aside soaring spears. Wild Horse saw the creature lurch towards a hunter who was climbing a tree, so that he might throw the spear that delivered the fatal wound. It was Dark Wolf, still trying to impress his older brother, Zuni. He was about to get himself killed.

He was also distracting the other hunters, giving Wild Horse a chance to escape.

But Wild Horse couldn't watch another death, especially one that he could prevent – and he was in the best position to inflict a fatal wound in the throat of the injured animal. He raised himself to stand on the branch. As the giant sloth raised its fore-limb to attack Dark Wolf, Wild Horse brandished his spear, shouting a hunting cry.

The giant sloth turned towards him, and so did the eyes of all the hunters.

Wild Horse threw his spear and it found its mark. The giant sloth bellowed, rage in its eyes as it heaved sideways and crashed to the ground.

Now shock began to ripple through the hunters as they recognised who had killed the sloth. Wild Horse and Zuni stared at each other, hatred blazing through both of them. Wild Horse had a raging desire to throw another spear, to pierce Zuni's throat, and he knew Zuni felt the same.

What had he done? Saved one life so that his own was now at risk?

Dark Wolf climbed down the tree and walked to his brother's side. He called out, 'I must thank you, Wild Horse. You risked your life to save mine. That is truly honourable. May the Spirits watch over you.'

Zuni did not take his eyes off Wild Horse, malevolence oozing from his dark, narrowed eyes. He gripped a spear so tightly it looked like he might crush it.

Wild Horse stood firm on the branch, and the other hunters looked at each other, not daring to speak.

At last Zuni said, 'Dark Wolf is right. You saved his life. You must come and join us for the feast to thank the Spirits for the good kill, and for my brother's life.'

'I have no wish to join you,' said Wild Horse.

'But you must,' Zuni bit back. 'It is our duty to honour you. And bring the girl. Come down.'

'What girl?'

'You know what girl. Blue Bird, daughter of Mogoll.'

'There is no girl with me,' said Wild Horse. 'As you can see, I am alone.'

'I don't believe you. I declared to Mogoll that I would find the girl and take her back.'

'You haven't found her. You've found me.'

'She's not far away. And she'll come looking for you. She'll want to know that you're safe.' Zuni leant against a tree, as if to show he'd wait there until Blue Bird arrived.

Wild Horse paused and thought hard. He'd never forget how Blue Bird had come looking for him when he had believed that he'd die after falling through the ice. Zuni was right: if he didn't return to her she was bound to come into the forest to find him. If he agreed to go with Zuni, it would give Blue Bird a chance to finish her journey on her own. At least she had Paska and Storm for company and she seemed to think that she didn't have that far to go. Once he was sure she'd got away, he would leave Zuni.

He climbed down. 'There is no girl. We parted some time ago. Anyway, aren't you too busy with your new wife to worry about pledges to Mogoll?'

The hunters, who had gathered round the lacerated body of their dead friend to chant to the Spirits, stopped and glanced at each other.

'Grab him!' shouted Zuni.

None of them moved.

'I am leader of this hunt. I said, grab him.'

There were too many for Wild Horse to fight. He was dragged through the tangle of undergrowth and pushed against a tree. Zuni bound his ankles and wrists, tightly to make sure the binding dug into Wild Horse's skin. Wild Horse refused to flinch, though he gritted his teeth and cursed deeply. Why had he chosen to save the life of Zuni's brother? He should have thrust his spear at Zuni instead of the giant sloth. Zuni would be dead.

But so would Dark Wolf.

'So much for honouring me,' he snarled. 'Is this how you repay me for saving Dark Wolf's life?'

'It's how I repay you for leaving me to die. I owe you nothing,' said Zuni, 'but as you did save my worthless brother, I won't kill you yet. I need you alive as my bait.

You say there is no girl, but I think you lie. She'll come.'

He walked off, telling one of the hunters to stay close to Wild Horse while the others butchered the sloth and he went to find a place to lay the body of the dead hunter.

It was Falcon – one of Mogoll's hunters – who stood over Wild Horse. It brought back memories of the bison stampede, Zuni walking back with the injured Falcon, telling the tale of Lightning's death. And all that followed. Too many bad memories. An uneasy silence fell between them, Wild Horse trying to ease the binding round his wrists without alerting Falcon.

Eventually Falcon said, 'Keep still.'

'What are you doing with Zuni?' Wild Horse asked the question that had been puzzling him. 'Did he join Mogoll's tribe after taking Night Rain as his wife?'

The hunter looked away.

'Surely you can tell me that.'

'Zuni has shown Mogoll that he is a fearless hunter. You saw his was the first spear to stab the giant sloth.'

'I also saw him lose another man. Zuni is a reckless hunter.'

Falcon crouched close to Wild Horse. 'You are still bitter that Zuni beat you. But know this: Zuni's bitterness runs deeper. He still doesn't have the wife.'

'Why not?'

'When we found him, bound as you are now, he said that he'd followed you and found the girl. But he had to admit to being beaten and Mogoll said he wasn't worthy to marry his daughter.'

That explained Zuni's rage, and the glances of the hunters when Wild Horse had mentioned Night Rain.

Wild Horse groaned. 'But why is he desperate to find Blue Bird?'

'Zuni asked Mogoll if there was another challenge for him, so that he might regain his honour. Mogoll told him that the first challenge remained, that if he found Blue Bird and brought her back, then Night Rain could become his wife.'

'What if the girl is already dead?'

Falcon sneered. 'Like Zuni, I think you lie and she lives, but Mogoll has no desire to make it easy for Zuni. If Zuni can't find her alive, Mogoll expects him to bring back some proof of her death.'

Wild Horse shuddered. He had to get back to Blue Bird before she came looking for him. The sun was barely visible through the trees as it started its descent.

'I'll take over the watch, Falcon.' Dark Wolf came towards them. 'Zuni says you'll want to help carry the body of our lost hunter. He has found a good place where it can wait for the Spirits to take the soul.'

Dark Wolf waited for Falcon and the other three hunters to pick up the body and follow Zuni before he knelt down beside Wild Horse.

'My brother does wrong by you. For the second time,' he said as he cut through the twine binding Wild Horse.

'It is a brave thing you do, Dark Wolf, but Zuni will make you suffer when he finds I'm gone,' said Wild Horse.

'I will suffer more, in here' – Dark Wolf thumped his

chest with his fist – 'if I don't do this. I've chased my brother's shadow for too long, but I now realise his shadow is too dark. You saved my life. Now I save yours. It is honourable.'

'What did you mean – *for the second time*?' asked Wild Horse, rubbing his wrists to be rid of the pain from the twine.

Dark Wolf looked at him steadily. 'It was Zuni who panicked the bison herd at the Sacred Rock. He told me it would be a clever tactic, but later I realised what harm it had caused you. I can't watch him harm you again.'

'Tall Tree and I knew that was what happened. I only wish my father had believed me. I must ask: why are you with Mogoll's hunters? Are you no longer with Bear Face?'

'There was bad blood between our fathers after you left. It was agreed that Great Wolf and I join Mogoll's tribe with Zuni.'

'That leaves Bear Face with few hunters,' said Wild Horse, wondering how his father felt about losing men from his tribe – his own brother Great Wolf among them.

Dark Wolf shook his head slowly. 'It was a sad day for me. I have not settled with Mogoll's people. There is a girl in our tribe – White Stone, daughter of Two Hawks – who was my friend.'

Wild Horse smiled. 'I remember White Stone. What are you going to do?'

'I have to show courage as you did, and leave my father. I will return to Bear Face, if he'll have me.'

'I'm sure he will, and if you tell him what happened at

Sacred Rock, maybe he will think better of me.'

'You could come back with me,' said Dark Wolf.

'No.' Wild Horse grabbed the young hunter's hand. 'I have my own journey ahead of me, but first I must do this.' He took a breath as he drew back his arm and let his fist fly into Dark Wolf's face.

Dark Wolf fell against a tree with a thud, clutching his jaw. 'Wild Horse! I free you and this is how you repay me.'

'It pained me, but it's the best way. Tell Zuni that I'd managed to wriggle out of my bonds, that I attacked you before escaping,' said Wild Horse, placing his hand on Dark Wolf's shoulder. 'Your face is bleeding so he should believe you.'

Dark Wolf nodded. 'You saw which way Zuni and the others took the body. Go now before they return. The Spirits go with you.'

'Thank you, cousin.' Wild Horse turned to leave. 'You must do what you think best, Dark Wolf, but if you want to make peace with my father and find happiness with White Stone, you could also leave now – before Zuni returns.'

Then he melted into the undergrowth, following the deer trail, hoping it would lead him back to the tree marks. Darkness was falling fast now, and he had to find his way back to Blue Bird before she set off to find him and found Zuni instead.

CHAPTER THIRTY-ONE

BLUE BIRD

Blue Bird paced in and out of the forest. If Wild Horse didn't appear soon she'd have to go looking for him, even though the light was dying.

At last he came running through the trees, nervously glancing over his shoulder, but with no kill over that shoulder. Something was wrong. Wild Horse wasn't just running towards her; he was running away from something, or someone.

'Quick, Blue Bird, we must put out that fire,' Wild Horse panted. 'It led me back to you, but it might lead others. We have to leave.'

'Who might it lead? What has happened?' A tremor shot through Blue Bird.

'Zuni, with hunters. I'll explain later, but we have to get away. He hunts for you – for us – in the forest.'

Wild Horse smothered the flames of Blue Bird's fire with the ferns. For a moment Blue Bird couldn't move. She stood dazed, looked at the doused fire, the woodpile, the swathes of ferns. All gone to waste. And what had happened to Wild Horse's face?

'The scar where the wolf attacked you,' she said, jolted out of her daze. 'It's torn open. Did Zuni do that to you?'

Just saying Zuni's name sent shivers across her shoulders as she heaved her sleeping-hide on to her back, her belongings still rolled up inside. *I must keep calm*, she told herself.

'No.' Wild Horse grabbed his hide roll.

'Who did, then?'

'There's no time to tell you now,' said Wild Horse. 'We must cross the Big River.'

She chased after him to the water's edge, Paska and Storm close behind.

Wild Horse splashed his face with the icy water, blood oozing over his hands.

Blue Bird scowled. 'There is much blood. Tell me who did that to you.'

'Not who, what. It was a sloth, a *giant* sloth. Come, we must hurry before . . . Shhh, did you hear that?'

The only thing Blue Bird could hear was her heart

pounding,

And a loud rustling sound from the trees behind them.

Getting closer.

There was no time to find a shallow crossing. The Big River was wide and waist-deep here, but they had to wade across it, Paska and Storm swimming beside them.

The water was so cold and her legs so wobbly that Blue Bird feared she wouldn't get across. She kept looking back to see if anybody, any*thing*, came running out of the forest. At least they weren't leaving any tracks.

As soon as they reached the other side they clambered up the riverbank. The forest on this side of the Big River was as dense as the side they'd just escaped from and they ran for cover, stopping to gaze back across the water as they caught their breath. Blue Bird couldn't stop shivering, and her wet leggings clung to her legs.

'Can you see anything?' she asked. 'Can you see Zuni?'

'No, but listen, I think I hear voices.'

Blue Bird tried to stop her teeth chattering as she strained to listen. There were sounds mingling with the rushing water. Yes, she did think they were voices.

Wild Horse took her hand. 'Are you ready? We must hurry.'

'Yes,' she said. Running would keep her warm.

They snaked through the trees, close to the edge of the forest, partly for the fading light, partly to glimpse any movement on the opposite riverbank. Neither of them spoke. The two animals moved quietly too, Paska at Blue Bird's heels, Storm close behind.

As the sun set behind them Blue Bird was glad of a clear sky with light from the stars and the moon. She was half running to maintain Wild Horse's pace, wiping the sweat from her forehead with the back of her hand, ignoring the pull of the muscles in her legs, concentrating on the rhythm of her hard breathing. No breath left to ask Wild Horse what else had happened. If only her legs were as long as his; it was difficult keeping up with him.

'Can we slow down?' she said at last, clutching her ribs. 'I have a deep ache.'

Wild Horse nodded, but he looked reluctant. 'We have covered much ground. With darkness falling we may be safe for now.'

'What makes you think Zuni would harm us if he did find us?'

'Zuni will not forgive us for how we left him,' said Wild Horse. 'He wants revenge for the shame he felt. Your father has told him he cannot have Night Rain until he finds us.'

He told Blue Bird about slaying the giant sloth, about Zuni binding him and Dark Wolf releasing him.

Blue Bird shook. 'So it was the giant sloth that tore your face? How big was it?'

Wild Horse pointed. 'As tall as that tree.'

Blue Bird was trying to imagine such a creature when she heard Paska whimpering a quiet warning. She froze. There was movement in the trees beyond the opposite riverbank, and once again, voices. Blue Bird and Wild Horse slowly lay flat on the ground. Peering through the undergrowth they saw Falcon run to the water's edge. The Big River was not quite as wide as where they crossed, but the current was much deeper and faster.

Falcon called, 'It's too deep to cross. He must still be in the forest.'

They waited for him to run back through the trees.

'We must leave the Big River,' said Wild Horse. 'If we stay by it we're more likely to see Zuni. We must turn away from the rising sun and go through the forest.'

Blue Bird was torn. The Big River had come to their rescue on the Great Plains, and it formed a barrier between them and Zuni, flowing hard and fast in the direction she wanted to take. The forest was so vast and deep they might easily become lost.

But she knew Wild Horse was right.

'Come on,' she said. 'Let's hope the forest swallows us up so that Zuni will never find us again.'

CHAPTER THIRTY-TWO

BLUE BIRD

It felt good to be leaving the Big River and Zuni behind.

Wild Horse said, 'This is the second time I find myself running away from my cousin with you by my side. Last time I wasn't sure if he'd come after us. This time I know he will.'

'We both know,' said Blue Bird.

'I'll make sure he doesn't take you back to Mogoll. I know you don't think you need protecting, but like Storm I will be fearless in the face of any danger that confronts us.' He snarled like the cub, a smile at the corner of his mouth.

'And Paska,' said Blue Bird. 'She proved she will protect me, *us*, when she bit Zuni's arm.'

'You're right. We have two fearless defenders.'

'It seems we are bound together, Wild Horse . . .'

They moved quickly to get as far from the Big River as possible, running deep into the night, using the light of the moon as it filtered through the tops of the trees. Blue Bird tried not to flinch at every rustle of undergrowth and snap of twig, every sound that could mean Zuni had followed them across the river. But they had no way of knowing where they were and the trees all looked the same in the dark. Blue Bird kept looking up at the stars, to make sure they weren't heading back towards the Big River. There was one very bright one surrounded by a cluster of tiny flickers. She hoped it was her mother's star, sent by the Spirits to guide them.

They came to a small clearing, where ancient trees had fallen, and decided it was a good place to make camp. There was plenty of dead wood to make a fire, but they didn't want any flames flickering through the night, flames that could bring Zuni to them. They agreed to take it in turns to keep watch.

Blue Bird felt the forest wrap around them, as if it was protecting them from Zuni. But it couldn't protect them against the danger of the predators that prowled among the trees at night.

It was so different from the Great Plains, which had

been so barren, so exposed with nowhere to hide. No predators, just the forces of nature, the thunderstorm, the howling wind, and no water. The forest offered many places to hide, and many animals, which filled the night air with noises: roars and shrieks, yelps and hoots, quiet scratching and crackling, and whimpers and wails – noises which could mask the sound of Zuni approaching with his hunters.

Blue Bird laid her arm over Paska, hoped the dog's senses would alert her, for Paska knew Zuni's scent, knew that he'd threatened her already. She was glad when the sky above her lightened, casting off the eeriness of the night.

They ate a little of the dried meat they had left and set off again, trying to keep the rays of light from the rising sun to their side. But sometimes the trees were so dense little light reached the forest floor. Blue Bird began to hunger for the endless sky of the plains.

'I have never been so deep in such a big forest,' she said. 'Mogoll always guided us round the edges.'

'It is too easy to get lost in such a place. That is why hunters do not care for it. But that is good for us. It will make it more difficult for Zuni to find us,' Wild Horse said.

It was this thought that kept Blue Bird going, though as they kept running she was constantly in fear of Zuni suddenly jumping out in front of her.

By the third sunset the fear of Zuni had begun to fade, but now she feared they were lost in the forest for ever. And they were hungry. The small springs and streams flowing between the trees meant they didn't run short of water, but they had eaten the last of the dried meat.

Dusk was a good time to hunt, so they made camp near a stream, gathering wood and lighting a fire before setting off with their spears.

Blue Bird called Storm to join them. 'It's time she helped with the kills. She eats more than we do.'

'Yes, she does,' said Wild Horse, but he didn't sound cross about it.

Blue Bird was the first to notice a path tunnelling through the undergrowth; it curled round to a stream. Pulling back the dense foliage they saw fresh droppings.

Wild Horse whispered, 'From the seeds in these droppings I think it's a tapir.'

They edged closer to the stream and there it was, a fully-grown animal, snout to the ground. Blue Bird and Wild Horse readied their spears. Then threw . . .

Both spears pierced the tapir's rear quarter and it squealed as it tried to drag itself away. Wild Horse was close behind, knife ready to finish the kill.

The dead animal was too heavy to drag back to the camp, so Wild Horse ran to get his tools while Storm tugged at a front leg, attacking it with her fangs, tearing at the flesh. It reminded Blue Bird of how long those fangs would grow, long enough to tear out a man's throat. She blinked away the image of Wild Horse's friend Tall Tree running towards the sabretooths. So much had happened since that day.

Wild Horse returned and cut off meat for the fire, then

severed a leg for Storm. 'If we leave the rest of the kill for the creatures that roam the night they won't need to bother us.'

'I'll take first watch,' said Blue Bird. 'I don't feel sleepy.'

Wild Horse was soon asleep, leaving Blue Bird alone with her thoughts. She was getting used to the forest, and to the calls and cries and hoots and howls of the night. And to listening for approaching hunters. The threat of Zuni still lurked in the back of her mind, still made her twitch at sudden sounds, and she wrapped her hand round her carved stick as she looked up through the leaves, hoping for a glimpse of the moon, wondering if they'd ever get out of the forest, if she'd still be here when it was time to cut the third notch.

The further they went, the more dense the trees grew, so that they couldn't see any sun the next day, making Blue Bird more anxious.

'It's hopeless,' she said. 'We're lost like we were on the Great Plains, but instead of too much grass there are too many trees.'

They had paused to fill their water-skins at a spring. Paska and Storm suddenly turned their heads, each murmuring a low growl. 'Danger,' said Blue Bird, readying her spear arm, sure it must be Zuni.

'I can't see or hear anything. Can you?' Wild Horse spun round.

'No, but I can feel something.'

Shadows skulking between the trees.

The hairs bristled on the back of her neck.

Eyes flickering in the gloom.

Teeth, bared teeth.

Not hunters, but animals emerging from between the trees. Blue Bird wasn't sure if she was relieved or more frightened.

'Dire wolves,' Wild Horse whispered.

'What should we do?' said Blue Bird. 'Run? Or attack? Can we frighten them off?' She brought back her spear arm, ready to throw.

'Not yet. Keep still,' said Wild Horse. 'We need to know how many there are; they usually roam in packs.'

'If you're working on a plan, then make it quick,' said Blue Bird, trying to keep the panic out of her voice.

They could run to the trees and climb, but it was too much of a risk against wolves. Anyway, although the cub could scramble up the tree, that would leave Paska helpless on the ground and Blue Bird wouldn't abandon her.

They could see eight wolves now, their ears drawn back, dark eyes glinting, large pointed teeth bared. They looked ready to attack . . .

There are too many of them, she thought, trying to hold her spear arm steady.

'This is what we must do,' whispered Wild Horse. 'The chief male rules the males in a pack, and his mate controls the females. If we kill the lead pair, the rest of the pack might run, or be content to feast from the dead meat of their leaders.'

'It's better than just waiting,' said Blue Bird. 'Are the

front two the leaders?'

'Yes. We just need to wait until they move a little closer, so that they are more in the open. The one closest to me is the male. You take the she-wolf by his side.'

'What?' hissed Blue Bird. 'We wait for them to get closer?'

'It's our best chance, so we mustn't miss with our first spears. And have your second and third ready in case the others come towards us.'

'And we've got our two defenders.' Blue Bird glanced at Paska and Storm. She wasn't sure how they could defeat the wolves, but somehow she scraped every bit of courage from every nerve in her body. She was proud to fight alongside Wild Horse.

Now was not the time for fear. Now was the time to fight for survival.

The lead wolves crept closer, but Blue Bird and Wild Horse were ready. Her spear flew towards the she-wolf at the same instant that his hurtled towards the muscular leader of the pack. The two creatures howled in pain and the others yelped in panic. It was their chance to frighten off the pack.

Blue Bird grabbed her second spear, her hand trembling.

Then human cries filled the air and many spears flew out from the surrounding trees.

Three wolves fell dead. The rest of the pack ran into the forest, baying, some with spear-points hanging from their bodies.

Blue Bird and Wild Horse looked at each other, their eyes wide with shock, hands tightly gripping their spears. Blue Bird felt like crying. Somehow Zuni and his hunters had found them. They'd been saved from the wolves only to be captured. She stood by Wild Horse, ready to challenge them, ready to throw her spear, ready to die rather than let Zuni drag her home.

CHAPTER
THIRTY-THREE

WILD HORSE

Wild Horse's spear was ready to be thrown straight into Zuni's throat. This time he would make sure the throw was fatal.

But it wasn't Zuni who came running out of the trees towards them. And Wild Horse didn't know any of the hunters.

There were seven of them: two men, one older boy and four of similar age to Wild Horse. They were all barefoot, most of them bare-chested, just wearing breechcloths over hide belts. Their hair hung loose, not braided like his and

Blue Bird's. Lengths of sinew hung round their necks, twisted with bits of bone and carved wood.

Wild Horse kept his spear ready.

'I am Red River, from the tribe of Bald Eagle,' said the older boy. He was tall and confident, probably two or three winters older than him. His black hair straggled over his shoulders, entwined with pieces of antler and feathers. 'You are strangers to this forest. May the Spirits be with you.'

Wild Horse pulled back his shoulders.

'I am Wild Horse, and this is Blue Bird,' he said. 'Your spears were true,' he added, respectfully. But he was still trying to accept what had happened: that they weren't facing Zuni and his hunters.

'As were yours, Wild Horse. You throw well.' The young hunter then turned to Blue Bird, smiling. 'And so do you, Blue Bird. Better than some of my men. I have never seen a girl hunt like that.'

Wild Horse saw how Blue Bird beamed back, letting the stranger hold her gaze.

'We did not mean to drive the pack in your direction,' said Red River, still looking at Blue Bird. 'I would do you no harm. We didn't know you were here.'

'Of course not,' said Blue Bird.

'Anyway, they were good kills. The tribe will eat well. And so will you. You must honour us by coming to our camp and joining the feast.'

'There's no need,' said Wild Horse. 'We have a long journey, don't we, Blue Bird?'

He looked at Blue Bird, expecting her to agree, but she glanced from him to Red River. 'Yes, but . . .'

'You helped with the kill,' Red River said with his head high. 'It is our duty to include you in the feast to praise the Spirits. I'll feel insulted if you do not feast with us, and my chief Bald Eagle will be displeased with me if I don't bring you to him so that he can thank you.'

'We have no wish to insult you,' said Blue Bird, 'or your chief. It will be an honour to come with you and meet him.'

'What about Storm?' asked Wild Horse, realising that the cub wasn't with them.

'The dog?' said Red River, looking at Paska. 'My sister has a dog; it is good.'

'Oh,' said Blue Bird, looking around, as if she'd forgotten about the cub. 'Storm?'

The cub dashed out of the forest towards her, blood dripping from her fangs. She'd obviously chased and caught up with one of the injured wolves.

Startled, the hunters readied their spears.

'Hold your spears,' shouted Wild Horse. 'She will not attack.'

But he could see that Red River and his hunters did not believe him. They stood close together, spears at shoulder height, as Blue Bird crouched next to the sabretooth, Paska on her other side.

'What have we here?' asked Red River.

'This is Paska,' said Blue Bird, 'and this is Storm. As you can see, Storm is no dog. Her dying mother gave birth in a cave I'd been sheltering in. Two other cubs died, but this little one survived. I thought she deserved a chance to live, so I am taking care of her until she is strong enough to return to the wild.'

'Not such a little one,' said Red River.

'Your hunters look scared,' said Wild Horse. 'It is best if we go our separate ways.'

'Wild Horse may be right,' said Blue Bird, looking up at Red River, 'though I promise that Storm wouldn't be a danger to your people.'

Red River looked from his hunters to the dead wolves, back to Blue Bird and the cub. 'You say the cat will not harm my people.'

'We will make sure she stays near us, won't we, Wild Horse?' replied Blue Bird. She smiled at Wild Horse, forcing him to smile back and say, 'Of course.'

'We watched your bravery when you confronted the wolves,' said Red River. 'Two of you against so many. You did not flinch when you threw your spears. You showed no fear. If my hunters are afraid of one sabretooth cub they should not be hunting. It is right that you return to our camp, you and both of your animals. It is right that you join us for the feast, to thank the Spirits for providing us with such good hunting, and for bringing us together.'

Wild Horse frowned, not ready to trust this hunter who had just burst into their lives. He'd spent so long alone with Blue Bird that the thought of feasting with others made him strangely ill at ease.

The legs of the wolves were tied so that each one could

be carried on a branch between two hunters, but the beasts were heavy so the journey to the tribe was slow. Red River bore the weight on his shoulders with ease as he walked with Blue Bird by his side. Wild Horse trailed behind with Storm.

The tribe's camp nestled in a large clearing, with a mountain range looming high above the forest. Wild Horse thought there were about twenty people in the tribe, like his own. Four children came to look at the cub, but their mothers pulled them away.

Chief Bald Eagle welcomed Blue Bird and Wild Horse. His greying black hair had a distinctive white streak, like the white feathers on the head of a bald eagle. He wore a sleeveless tunic of light deerskin over his breechcloth, and a wide sinew strip round his neck adorned with eagle claws and feathers. He found them a place on the outer edge of the camp where they could put up a shelter, close enough to feel the safety of kinship, but far enough away for Storm to be less of a worry to the tribe.

As Wild Horse and Blue Bird unrolled their hides Wild Horse said, 'I hope you didn't tell Red River about Zuni. We should not bother him with our troubles.'

'I didn't tell Red River, but maybe I should, in case Zuni comes looking for us and threatens his people.'

'We'll be on our way soon after sunrise, so there should be no danger for the tribe.'

'But he might not find us. We travelled for many nights through the forest. We were close to being savaged by a pack of wolves.' Blue Bird's eyelids fluttered at the memory. 'Their hunters rescued us, Wild Horse. We might be safe here.'

'We might,' he said, not wanting to see her fear again.

'So there is no rush to leave.'

'I suppose not,' said Wild Horse. He wanted to believe that they'd be safe, that Zuni would not come this way. Their tribe had never ventured this far, so his cousin would most likely follow the course of the Big River they'd left behind, knowing that it led to the Great River which Sacred Cloud had told them they had to cross. *But if Zuni didn't find them there . . .*

'Red River did ask why we travelled alone,' Blue Bird said.

'What did you say?'

'That you had run away from your tribe, as I had left mine. That you chose to join me in my quest to find my mother's people, and we'd decided it was safest to journey together.'

'What else did you say? You talked for long enough.'

'I asked him about his people. His father is dead – killed last winter – his mother is called Red Deer and he has three sisters: Swift, Little Lion and Feather. Red River is fifteen winters old, and he is named for the Big River that we left behind.'

'What?' said Wild Horse.

Blue Bird laughed. 'I told him about the Big River we found when we were trying to cross the Great Plains, and he said his tribe call it Red River.'

'Why?'

'It's from a tale told by his father's father. Hunters from several tribes stampeded a huge herd of bison over a cliff into the river – there was much killing. They said the river wept red with blood for many a moon afterwards.'

'Does the tribe still go to the Big River?' asked Wild Horse.

'You mean Red River.' Blue Bird smiled. 'Not really. They spend most of the time around this forest. They usually spend three or four moons at this camp, after the Snow Moons, and there is another one downriver where they will spend the next three or four moons.'

'That is a long time to stay in one camp,' said Wild Horse.

'Red River says that it is a good place, which is why they come back to it. They know the forest well. There are deer as well as wolves here, and mountain lions and sabretooths on the other side of a nearby river called the Falling River. And, of course, plenty of wood from the trees to make spears and fore-shafts.' Blue Bird smiled at Wild Horse. 'And there is good chert nearby. We both need more points, Wild Horse. Why don't we stay longer? Red River says we can stay as long as we like, and . . . I feel . . .'

'What?'

Blue Bird shrugged. 'Safe.'

'It's your journey,' Wild Horse said.

'*Our* journey, Wild Horse. We have the protection of a whole tribe. Don't you think it will be best to stay with them until we're sure the threat of Zuni has passed? To wait until we're sure he hasn't tracked us through the forest?' She paused. 'But if you believe it will be safer to keep going we'll set off at sunrise.'

'You're probably right,' mumbled Wild Horse.

'It will be good,' she said.

The whole tribe sat round the campfires for the feast, the fires hissing and spluttering as fat and blood dripped from the cooking wolf carcasses on to the flames. Smoke curled upwards, carrying the aromas of the roasting flesh, and Bald Eagle called loud praises to the Spirits. Everybody raised their arms up to the darkening sky.

But Wild Horse fidgeted, feeling oddly alone. He sat on the far side of the fire-pits, managing to ignore the chatter of the people around him, while Blue Bird seemed to enjoy the babble and bustle, chatting to Red River and his eldest sister. Wild Horse hoped she didn't notice him slip away.

CHAPTER THIRTY-FOUR

WILD HORSE

The sun was tingeing the treetops with a glimmer of light when Wild Horse set off into the forest. Blue Bird had stayed at the feast until very late and was still asleep. Storm was by his side. It was time the sabretooth learnt how to stalk and kill its own prey, something the mother cat would have shown her cubs.

Wild Horse decided it was time for Storm to learn – and she would have to learn quickly, or she'd never survive in the wild. The young sabretooth's instincts at stalking were good, but she didn't time it well, often jumping up for the kill too soon or leaping in the wrong direction. Wild Horse supposed the mother would teach her young by pushing them to copy her body movements as they hunted together. He couldn't do that, so he'd have find another way.

A picture of Blue Bird with Paska filled his mind. Sometimes the dog responded to calls, but Blue Bird used hand signals when they were hunting. He wondered if it would work with Storm. It was worth trying.

They stayed in the forest all day, and by the end of it Storm had helped him bring down a deer much bigger than herself. Wild Horse had injured the deer to slow it down, by throwing a spear into a leg, then with just one hand signal – repeated again and again – he'd directed the cub to cross the path of the wounded animal and to make the kill.

He had allowed Storm to feed before slinging the carcass over his shoulders – it would be good to return to the camp to show off the cub's kill.

The tribespeople kept their distance as Wild Horse walked back in with Storm by his side. It suited him; he didn't need to get close to anybody. He'd just enjoyed the freedom to do what he wanted to do. Hunting with the young sabretooth had been good, and he decided that he would do it each day while they stayed with Bald Eagle's tribe. He could learn more about animals as he taught Storm. And he could look out for Zuni too, though with every day that passed he felt the memory of his cousin fading.

When he told Blue Bird about Storm's kill she was excited and Wild Horse realised he'd missed her. 'You can join us tomorrow,' he said.

'I'd love to,' said Blue Bird, 'but Swift is going to show me the plants they collect from the forest floor. They are quite different from those I know as they don't get much light.'

Wild Horse was disappointed, but tried not to show it.

The next day he and Storm went hunting deeper into the forest. Blue Bird leapt up to greet them when they returned to camp.

'I've been digging up roots, and grinding,' she said, happily. 'Some of my tools are old and need replacing. I wondered if you'd join Red River and the hunters when they go to the ridge for chert tomorrow, and fetch some for me.'

'Yes,' said Wild Horse, 'and I need new points, but you'll have to watch Storm. At least there is plenty to feed her.'

'Of course. And Paska will stay with her. Though she has become friendly with Swift's dog. It's the first time she's seen another dog, since she was abandoned.'

'Don't let the other dog get close to Storm. She has to return to the wild,' Wild Horse said abruptly, feeling the need to remind Blue Bird.

He was pleased she'd asked him to get chert, and not Red River.

The next morning the early sun cast a glow over their shoulders as the band of hunters walked towards the flint ridge.

'It is good fine-grain stone,' said Red River. 'Mostly grey, but you will find seams of green and yellow. There are boulders nearby we use to strike the edge of the large flint core.'

Wild Horse nodded, not really wanting to talk.

'It's a place we come back to,' Red River continued. 'We chip off large flakes that we can make into many tools. What do you need, Wild Horse? Spear-points, I suppose, and maybe a new knife blade.'

'And for Blue Bird,' said Wild Horse. 'Her tools are well used and blunted. She asked me to bring back some chert.'

'I will make sure you find her the finest flakes,' said Red River. 'She has so much skill. And she brings much pleasure to my sister – and to me.'

'Yes,' was all Wild Horse could reply. He stood at the top of the ridge, gazing at the forest spreading far into the distance. *If Zuni and the hunters were approaching, would I be able to see them from here?* Looking the other way, he could see a wide river beyond the camp, sweeping a broad course through the forest.

'That is the Falling River,' said Red River. 'It comes a long way from the mountains, with many steep waterfalls upriver. You can see one in the distance,' he pointed. 'As the water plunges over a steep overhang, watch how the spray rises like white horses charging from the depths.'

'It does,' said Wild Horse.

Red River glanced at Wild Horse, 'Or should I say like

wild horses, as I am with a brave hunter who is named for such a fine creature?'

Wild Horse wasn't sure what to say. He was relieved when Red River went on: 'As you can see, below us the river is wider and shallower. There are fewer falls as it winds its way down to the Great River.'

Wild Horse wondered how far it was to the Great River when a flicker of movement caught his attention. *Antlers?* He wondered what hunting there might be in the forest on the other side of the Falling River. *And better hiding places from Zuni?*

'I still remember the way Blue Bird threw her spear at the she-wolf, like a true hunter,' Red River smiled. 'She has the eyes of a hunter, doesn't she? Very good eyes.'

'Oh,' said Wild Horse, shaking the image of Zuni out of his head, 'yes, very good eyes,' and he remembered how he'd first been gripped by Blue Bird's eyes, not quite green, not quite brown.

'She told me that she trained her young brothers how to throw a spear. I have asked her to teach the young ones in the tribe,' said Red River. 'Little Lion and Feather, my two younger sisters. And Bald Eagle's youngest son, Black Fox. And Raven, who is the son of Hook Nose, my best hunter.'

'And did she say that she would?' asked Wild Horse. If Blue Bird wanted to stay longer with the tribe, what would that mean for him? And for Zuni? Looking down over the forest made him think: had they come far enough through the forest to lose him?

CHAPTER THIRTY-FIVE

BLUE BIRD

'I think the Spirits sent Bald Eagle's tribe to us,' said Blue Bird. They were sitting outside their shelter, resting. Blue Bird was cutting a fourth notch on her stick – another full moon had passed last night.

'What do you mean?' asked Wild Horse.

'First Red River's hunters appeared out of the darkness of the forest to save us from the wolves. Now we have the protection of a tribe and plenty to eat, and there is chert to flake. When Red River asked if I'd train the children with spears, I thought it would be a good way to repay them for making us so welcome. And while I've been doing that it has given you more time to train Storm.'

She looked at her stick thoughtfully.

'Red River says that when they move to the next camp where they spend several moons, they will follow the course of the Falling River. It flows towards the sunrise, and it will be good to travel with them for a while.'

Wild Horse said, 'So we will continue our journey to find your family?'

'Yes . . .' said Blue Bird, but suddenly she wasn't sure. 'Don't you feel safer knowing we are not alone?'

Wild Horse shrugged, looked uneasy.

'Do you still think about Zuni?'

Now he looked shocked. 'Yes,' he said, 'but . . .'

A cloud of silence hung over them.

'Wild Horse?' It was Red River, striding towards them. 'I've watched you in the forest, hunting with the cat.'

Blue Bird was glad of the interruption, and she could sense Wild Horse was too.

'The way you pick up trails, the way you listen for sounds, and sniff at droppings to find out how fresh they are . . . It is good. You know so much. How do you do it?'

'Instinct, training,' replied Wild Horse, 'but mostly I've learnt from watching the animals. They've taught me well.'

'Are you willing to share the knowledge with us?' said Red River. 'Could we join you and the sabretooth when you hunt?'

'You already hunt well,' said Wild Horse. 'You know the forest. What could I show you?'

'Your tracking skills are better.'

'And your words are generous,' said Wild Horse, 'but I fear that hunting with many humans will not be right for the sabretooth.'

Blue Bird said, 'I can hunt with Storm and you can join Red River and the hunters.'

'Yes, that would be good,' said Red River.

Wild Horse said, 'But you haven't hunted for some time and you don't know the signals I've taught Storm.'

'So I'll hunt with you first and you can show me.' Blue Bird spoke firmly, not allowing Wild Horse to say no.

They set off early with Storm the next sunrise, and quickly fell back into their old ways of hunting together. Blue Bird realised how much she missed it. As they scurried through the undergrowth, looking for tracks, Wild Horse showed her the signals he'd taught Storm.

They walked back to the camp talking and laughing, the cub behind them, her jaws firmly gripping a young wolf. She settled down to devour it under some trees.

'It's her first kill without my help,' Wild Horse told Red River. 'She didn't even need the signals.'

Red River put his hand on Wild Horse's shoulder. 'That is proof of how good you are, Wild Horse. Now you can train us to track as well as you've trained the sabretooth.'

Blue Bird wanted to throw her arms round both of them, but didn't. It would be good for Wild Horse and Red River to hunt together.

*

When Wild Horse led the hunters into the forest Blue Bird left Paska with Storm as she took the younger children and Swift to a small clearing for the spear practice. As they walked Swift told Blue Bird that her brother talked about her all the time, and Blue Bird laughed because she didn't know what else to do.

The sun was low in the sky by the time the hunters returned.

'It was difficult hunting,' said Red River. 'We had to travel far to find anything. All the trails were old, until Wild Horse smelt fresh horse dung.'

'But the horses bolted and it took all our efforts to catch and kill one. Your hunters run well,' said Wild Horse.

At last Wild Horse and Red River speak well of each other, thought Blue Bird, *so we can stay with the tribe a while longer until we are sure Zuni won't find us.*

Red River sat down on a log, smearing blood from his hands on to the bark. 'There is little prey close by, but Wild Horse thinks he saw elk on the other side of the Falling River when we stood on the chert ridge . . .'

CHAPTER THIRTY-SIX

WILD HORSE

Wild Horse was glad to try new hunting grounds, especially as Storm was growing fast and needed more food. He wondered how long she could live on the outskirts of their camp. He knew that if Storm was ever going to survive in the wild, he had to make sure she didn't become too tame.

They found many elk in the forest on the other side of the Falling River. The meat had strong flavour and the antlers made fine tools. Bald Eagle asked the shaman to send special thanks to the Spirits. It was good hunting and they returned several times, but after another moon it was time to move on.

They walked by the Falling River for four days, making brief overnight stops, passing a steep waterfall where they watched the sunrise cast a shimmering glow over the tumbling water. Finally they reached the place where the tribe always stayed for three or four moons, while the trees and bushes were laden with berries and nuts. The camp was made in a clearing at the edge of the forest, not far from the river.

There were many fish in the river, and sometimes Blue Bird and the children followed Red River to the water's edge where they fished together. Wild Horse watched him – he'd never seen anybody who could grab a fish out of the water with such speed, and his respect for Red River grew. He was a powerful hunter too. He might not have Wild Horse's tracking instincts, but his spear arm was strong and his aim was true.

One day Red River asked him, 'What creature gave you such a scar on your chin? It is the sign of a good hunter, for you lived and the animal must surely have died.'

Wild Horse told him about the wolf fight in the frozen river, but didn't say anything about the giant sloth. He didn't want to start talking about what had happened with Zuni, didn't want to admit that his own cousin wanted to kill him and capture Blue Bird.

Red River remained the tribe's lead hunter, but Wild Horse used his skills to find hoof marks and trails, any traces of prey. He was getting to know the other hunters, particularly the three younger ones: Bald Eagle's older son Eye of the Owl – often called Owl – who was twelve winters, and the two brothers Black Hawk and White Crow, whose parents had both died last winter. Black Hawk had seen thirteen winters like Wild Horse with White Crow the younger by one winter.

Wild Horse suggested they try hunting on the other side of the Falling River again, in case the elk had moved downriver too. Deep in the forest he found tracks, and he crouched down to the woodland floor, tensing as he realised they belonged to a sabretooth. Apart from Storm he hadn't seen any of the big cats since the hunt that had ended in the death of Tall Tree.

Was there just one? Or several planning an ambush?

Then he saw a sturdy female prowling between the trees ahead of them. The forest thinned out as the hunters followed the sabretooth to see if other cats joined it, keeping their distance, not close enough to throw their spears. They came to a stream, burbling between rocks – and there they were.

Two more female sabretooths with two cubs, all tearing at the flesh of a large elk.

Red River signalled to the hunters to be still and Wild Horse breathed deeply. As he closed his eyes for the briefest moment, to blot out the vision of his dead friend, he saw what to do, and he picked up a small boulder.

'I'll throw this to land between the walking cat and the ones that feast. It should scare her back towards us, and if the Spirits are with us, the others will flee across the stream.'

'Our spears are ready,' said Red River.

And so it was. Red River's eyes sparkled after the kill, and he praised Wild Horse all the way back to the camp.

'But it was your spear brought it down,' said Wild Horse.

'And it was your boulder that scared the cat. My spear could not miss such a ready target.'

Back at the camp Bald Eagle said, 'The Spirits blessed the tribe when they brought you to us, Wild Horse. You find the hunters good kills.'

The rest of the tribe murmured in agreement. Wild Horse walked away to his shelter – the praise made him feel awkward. He wasn't used to it. He sensed Blue Bird almost before she spoke.

'You have done well,' she said, 'but I fear that Storm might sense it is one of her own kind that is being butchered.'

'She looks as if she's too busy enjoying her own kill,' said Wild Horse.

'I hope so. She brought down a fawn and dragged it back here when I took her hunting.'

Wild Horse watched the cub, thinking about what he'd seen. He felt Blue Bird's gaze on him.

'Is there something troubling you, Wild Horse?'

'There were two other female big cats, and two young, so there may be a male nearby. I wonder if he would accept another female – a young lost female . . .'

'Storm?' Blue Bird's voice faltered. 'I don't think she's ready. She's too young. She still doesn't go hunting on her own. Do you think she's ready?'

'I don't know, but we should give her the chance.'

'But they might attack her,' said Blue Bird.

'I know, but they might not. It might be her best chance of returning to the wild. Her only chance, especially if we stay with the tribe any longer.'

Wild Horse waited for Blue Bird's response, but she said nothing.

'If she stays here with us she'll get too used to humans.'

Blue Bird's green-brown eyes glistened as she blinked back tears. 'So we need to journey to find my family and take Storm with us, or find her a family?'

'I didn't mean it to sound like that,' said Wild Horse. 'I was thinking what's best for Storm. Maybe we should enjoy the feast and talk about it later.'

CHAPTER THIRTY-SEVEN

BLUE BIRD

It was a good feast, with much talk about the sabre-tooth fangs and teeth. The younger children made up a game where they scattered the teeth on the ground. In turn each child threw one tooth up, then had to grab as many of the other teeth in their hand as possible, and catch the thrown tooth before it hit the ground. The winner was the child who had the most teeth in their hand.

It was Little Lion, and she jumped up and down when Bald Eagle declared the prize would be the two fangs.

Blue Bird smiled at the sound of their laughter, but she found it difficult to enjoy herself. She couldn't stop thinking about Storm.

'Again Wild Horse found us good prey,' said Red River, who was sitting next to her. 'He told us how the sabretooths work together to ambush their prey, and he showed us how to separate them.'

Red River's words reminded Blue Bird that the last time Wild Horse had been part of a sabretooth kill it had led to the death of Tall Tree. It must have been difficult for him, and yet he had come back speaking of what to do with Storm, and whether it was time to leave the tribe.

'I enjoyed hunting with Wild Horse,' Red River said, his hand brushing hers. 'But it is good to be by your side as we feast. I have grown fond of you, Blue Bird.'

His words seemed to hover over her.

Red River leant closer to her. 'You seem quiet. What troubles you?'

'Nothing,' she said. 'It's good to be by your side too.'

But her thoughts were with Wild Horse. She watched him leave the feast and walk towards their shelter.

She told Red River she was tired, then said a few words to Swift before crawling into the shelter. Wild Horse lay still, but she knew he wasn't asleep.

'Wild Horse?' She patted his shoulder and he turned. 'I think . . . you're right. About Storm. She deserves a chance to meet the sabretooth pack.'

Wild Horse sat up. 'Are you sure?' he said. 'What if *you're* right and they attack her?'

'I've thought of nothing else since you told me,' said Blue Bird, 'and I couldn't eat. Storm has more chances of surviving in a pack than on her own.'

'It's a brave decision, Blue Bird,' said Wild Horse, 'I'll set off with Storm at sunrise.'

'No,' said Blue Bird, '*We'll* set off *before* sunrise. I want to be away before the rest of the camp awakes.'

'Why? Red River will wonder where we've gone. You stay here.'

'No,' Blue Bird insisted. '*I* was the one who saved her. I want to be with her – with you – when we set her free. It is right. It should be the three of us.'

'Three? What about Paska?'

'I spoke to Swift at the end of the feast, asked if I could leave Paska with her while we took Storm to the sabre-tooths. I told her that we'd be gone by the time she woke.'

'And Red River?'

'I asked Swift not to tell him until he realised I'd gone. I knew he'd want to come too.'

Wild Horse's smile told her how pleased he was that they'd be going alone.

And after a little fitful sleep they were on their way – spears at the ready, Storm by their side. Blue Bird thought the young cub seemed suddenly smaller, not old enough for a life in the wild. She asked the Spirits to guide them.

The camp was near a shallow part of the Falling River which they could cross easily. In the quiet of the night they could hear the faint sound downriver where it swelled deeper, crashing over rocks before plunging over a craggy waterfall. They entered the forest with no light to guide them, just glimpses of the stars and moon peeking between the treetops.

Wild Horse said, 'It's still too dark to pick up the hunters' tracks in the undergrowth, or the marks I made on trees. I hope I can remember the right direction.'

'Of course you can,' Blue Bird smiled. Wild Horse always knew the way.

It felt good to have him by her side, just the two of them once more. As the first shafts of sunlight filtered through the branches Wild Horse told Blue Bird that Red River talked of her often.

'Does he?' she said, trying to hide a smile, not admitting that Swift had told her the same.

'Do you want to know what he says?'

'Only if it's good.'

'Of course it's good,' said Wild Horse.

He joked about how he got sick of hearing Red River going on about her, mimicked his voice, carried on teasing her until she laughed and told him to stop. But Blue Bird was happy – Wild Horse had accepted her friendship with Red River.

The sun was nearing its highest point when Wild Horse recognised the place where they'd made the kill.

'See the vultures,' he said. 'They've probably found the remains of the elk that the sabretooths had brought down.'

Flies buzzed round the elk corpse, but there was no sign

of the sabretooths.

'I suppose the big cats have taken as much meat as their fangs would allow, leaving plenty for the scavengers,' said Wild Horse. 'There's most likely a herd of elk around here, but I can't see where the sabretooths went next.'

'I think Storm has picked up their scent,' said Blue Bird. 'See how she sniffs round the carcass.'

'You're right. She's on the trail of something.'

They followed the cub, spears raised, both looking out for droppings or paw prints. Storm tensed as she hunkered down, ears twitching, and Blue Bird shivered as she looked at Wild Horse. He'd sensed it too. Without a word they both crouched behind rocks and watched as a sabretooth prowled towards a waterhole from the opposite direction and started to drink. There was blood round its mouth from a fresh kill.

Blue Bird and Wild Horse edged closer, and further along, at the edge of the treeline, they saw another three sabretooths gorging on a large elk with magnificent antlers.

This was Storm's chance. The cub hadn't eaten since the previous sunset, so she would be hungry enough to be lured by the scent of blood and flesh. It was a large beast so there should be enough meat for another, if the pack allowed it.

Storm stayed where she was, low and watchful. It wasn't until one of the adult sabretooths pulled away from the carcass and walked to the waterhole that she started to creep towards the kill.

The sabretooths looked up and Storm stopped.

'Go on, Storm,' Blue Bird whispered. 'Be brave. Go on.' She felt Wild Horse lightly take hold of her hand and looked at him. 'I can't watch, Wild Horse. What if they attack her?'

'They won't,' he murmured, but he didn't sound sure.

CHAPTER THIRTY-EIGHT

WILD HORSE

Wild Horse tried to sound convincing, but his heart was in his throat as Storm crept to the head of the carcass and began ripping at the flesh round the neck. Blue Bird squeezed his hand so hard he nearly cried out. A large male strode forwards, flanked by two females. It raised its head and snarled, a low warning growl.

Wild Horse froze. He knew that if Storm had been a male then death would be certain – a dominant male wouldn't accept a male cub from another father. But Wild

Horse hoped that this male, having lost one of his females, might be ready for another female to join the pack.

Storm backed away a little when she heard the male roar, but didn't run. As the male sank its fangs into the rump of the elk Storm crept back and started eating again. The two females returned to the carcass, and soon Wild Horse and Blue Bird were watching the six animals ravaging the flesh.

After some time Wild Horse signalled to Blue Bird that they must go.

'I don't want to leave Storm,' murmured Blue Bird.

'We have to,' he whispered. 'You can see she's been accepted. It's too risky to stay here, for her as well as for us.'

He pulled her away, but she kept looking back. When they had reached what he thought was a safe distance he let go of her hand. Her eyes were damp with tears and he blinked back his own as he put his hands on her shoulders.

'Blue Bird. You know what we've done is the right thing. Storm needs to be with her own kind. We must let her go.'

'I know,' she said, as she crumpled to the ground, 'but they might still attack her.'

'We've done all we can. It's up to her now. She is strong and clever. We must be proud.'

'Please, can we stay here awhile? Just in case they frighten her away. Give her a chance to come after us.'

Wild Horse knew that if they wanted to get back to the camp by sunset they should set off, but he could see how upset Blue Bird was. They walked along the treeline and found a hollow where they could sit unseen. A breeze rustled through the long grasses, and they sat and watched how it bent the fronds back and forth like a wave; they were both lost in their own thoughts.

And then they talked about Storm: how helpless she'd been at the start of their journey, how much Wild Horse really didn't want her at first, how she'd won him round.

'I will always be grateful to you,' said Blue Bird, 'as will Storm. I think she won't forget you.'

'Or you,' he said.

A flight of geese honked overhead, and Wild Horse realised the breeze had strengthened into a wind. Clouds were scudding towards them from the mountains and the sky was darkening.

'A storm approaches,' he said to Blue Bird. 'We'd best stay here. At least this hollow offers some cover.' The rain lashed down in torrents, forcing them to squeeze together at the back of the hollow, and Wild Horse suddenly laughed.

'What's funny?'

'I was thinking of the last storm we were in, and how it gave Storm her name.'

'At least we know she's not frightened,' said Blue Bird. 'Well, not of the storm, but we don't know if the pack will end up scaring her away.'

'It's just as well the storm came then,' he said, knowing how much it would please her. 'By the time it passes it will be too dark to travel safely through the forest, so if she doesn't settle with the pack it gives her extra time to come and find us.'

'Thank you, Wild Horse, and to the Spirits for sending the storm.'

Wild Horse was also glad of the storm. It gave him longer with Blue Bird – he realised he didn't enjoy sharing her with the rest of the tribe.

'Do you ever think about Zuni?' she asked.

Wild Horse sighed. 'Our tribe has never come this far,' which was true. 'But,' he added, not wanting Blue Bird to take any risks, 'that doesn't mean we shouldn't be vigilant. It isn't Zuni's nature to give up.'

They chatted until there was no light in the sky. With no sleeping-hides, no fire and little space, they huddled together through the night, taking it in turns to keep watch.

The clouds were gone and the rising sun warmed their faces as they set off into the forest in the morning. There was no sign of the sabretooths.

'I think Storm has settled with her new family,' Wild Horse said out loud, to himself as much as Blue Bird. 'If they'd chased her off she'd have found us by now.'

A soft silence fell between them as they walked through the forest. Blue Bird paused from time to time, stroking trees and rocks. 'To leave my scent for Storm, just in case . . .' she said.

Wild Horse found himself looking over his shoulder, to check if the cub was following them. She was very young and he hoped that she had the strength to survive without them, but he'd miss her very much, miss their moments hunting together.

As they emerged from the trees, to cross back over the Falling River, Wild Horse looked at Blue Bird. He wanted to say so many things. *We found a family for Storm – what about your family?*

'We did it,' was all he managed. Before she could answer a shout rang across the water. It was Swift.

'Praise the Spirits you're back,' she cried. 'You must hurry!'

CHAPTER THIRTY-NINE

BLUE BIRD

Swift grasped Blue Bird's hand as she clambered up the riverbank. Her eyes were filled with tears. 'Blue Bird, I have done all I can, and so has our mother, but Red River has lost much blood. He is very weak.'

'What happened?' Blue Bird's chest tightened with fear.

'When I told him what you and Wild Horse were doing with Storm he wanted to set off after you. He thought he could help. If only I'd let him go, he wouldn't be hurt, though...' Swift shuddered.

'Though what, Swift?' said Blue Bird.

'He saved Little Lion. My sister is safe, but I may lose my brother.'

'No, that can't be true!' Her whole body trembled as she darted between trees, chasing Swift, vaguely aware that Wild Horse ran beside her.

A droning sound drifted towards them as they neared the camp. Instantly Blue Bird knew what it was: the shaman calling the Spirits.

'Don't get any louder,' she begged, knowing that a shaman wailed loudest when a person died, to ward off evil Spirits as the soul leaves the body.

When they reached the camp she was gasping for breath, and waited for some moments outside Red River's shelter. Wild Horse briefly squeezed her hand.

'I'll wait here,' he said.

Blue Bird blinked away tears when she saw how badly Red River's thigh was slashed open. She knelt down and took his hand. *How could a hand feel so cold when his forehead was sweaty with fever?*

'I'm glad you're back,' he whispered, his eyelids fluttering. 'I wanted to see you before the Spirits take me.'

'It's not your time to be taken,' she said, gulping for air. 'I'm here to look after you.'

'My leg. It's too bad.' Red River's face twisted as he spoke.

Blue Bird took a deep breath and looked closer at the wound, tried not to flinch. Bare bone covered in blood, pus oozing at ragged edges.

Swift murmured, 'We tried to clean the wound, but he screamed from the pain, told us to stop. I could not add to his suffering. And he told our mother that she should be with our sisters, that they need her more than he does. Little Lion is very upset – she thinks it's her fault.'

'She must not think so,' said Red River. He tried to pull himself up, but fell back.

'What happened?' asked Blue Bird. She held his hand tightly.

Red River spoke quietly. 'We were fishing . . . Little Lion wandered off . . . to gather flowers. She screamed . . . A huge bull mastodon . . .' He closed his eyes as if to blot out the vision. 'She was too scared to move . . . I ran . . . threw her out of the way. But . . .'

Swift took his other hand. 'The mastodon gored him and hurled him into the air.'

Blue Bird felt her eyes fill with tears. No wonder the wound was so jagged, so deep. She wasn't sure how much she could do, and the thought of worsening his pain stung her, but she had to try.

'I'll get what I need. You stay with your brother,' she said to Swift, and ran from the shelter.

'How is he?' asked Wild Horse, leaving the group of hunters he'd been talking to.

'It's very bad.' She walked quickly towards their shelter, still trying not to cry. 'I've never seen such a terrible wound.'

'Is there anything I can do?' asked Wild Horse.

'I need my balm and fresh water. And some sinew. Do

you know what happened?'

'Yes, White Crow told me how brave Red River was. The beast was whirling round in a frenzy,' Wild Horse said as he helped her collect what she needed. 'The way White Crow described its deep rumbling like distant thunder makes me think it was a bull desperate to mate. It can make them lose control and become very aggressive. I've seen it happen once, when I was about seven winters old.'

'You must have been very frightened,' said Blue Bird.

'We all were, but Bear Face recognised the rumble that White Crow heard. He moved the tribe out of their shelters just in time and the rampaging bull tore through one shelter, then kept digging its tusks into the ground. My father said it was rage, but it looked to me like it was also in pain – there was thick pus bleeding out of a hole between its eye and ear.'

Blue Bird grimaced. She didn't want to hear about mastodon pus. She had Red River's to cope with. 'I must get back,' she said. 'Is Little Lion all right?'

'The little one is blessed. Her brother threw her into the arms of Water Snake, just before the beast tossed him into the air. Low bushes broke his fall. If he'd landed on rocks his whole body would be broken.'

Blue Bird shuddered. If the Spirits had not let Red River fall on to rocks maybe they'd let him live so that she could heal him. She silently appealed to the Spirits to help her as Wild Horse asked if she needed anything else.

'One thing,' said Blue Bird. 'There is a plant with purple flowers that has a thick black root.'

'I know the plant. It's good to chew the root if you've got toothache.'

'That's right, but it's good for help healing wounds too. My balm is made from it, but I don't have enough.'

'Where will I find it?'

'It does not like shade, so rarely seen near a forest,' she said. 'There is more open woodland and rocks downriver towards the waterfall,' said Wild Horse. 'White Crow and Black Hawk will help me. They carried Red River back here and they'll do anything to help him. We'll do our best to find it.'

They set off and Blue Bird took a deep breath before entering the shelter of Red River once more.

He was very brave, but she saw the pain in his eyes as she washed out the pus and smeared balm round the edges of the wound. Finally she loosely tied a length of sinew round the leg, to hold the flap of skin in place. Red River fell into a deep sleep and Swift said that Red Deer, their mother, would like to sit with him.

Blue Bird crawled out of the shelter to be greeted by Paska. It was a relief to sit on the ground and stroke the dog. It reminded her of Storm. She gazed up at the sky and pleaded with the Spirits to look after the cub and Red River, to keep them both in this world.

CHAPTER FORTY

WILD HORSE

'Blue Bird, look what we've brought you!' Wild Horse walked quickly, with White Crow and Black Hawk close behind.

'Our mother was good at healing, like you,' said White Crow.

'When she died we kept the medicines that she stored in this pouch.' Black Hawk handed it to Blue Bird. 'We didn't know what most of them were.'

'When we set off with Wild Horse to look for the plant with purple flowers it didn't mean much,' said White Crow, 'until he mentioned it had a black root. We came back straight away. Open it!'

Wild Horse watched Blue Bird pull out the dried black root from the pouch, enjoyed the unexpected delight brighten her face.

White Crow was excited. 'We'd forgotten all about it, but our mother used it for cuts and snake bites, many things.'

'Your mother was very wise,' said Blue Bird, 'like my aunt, Sacred Cloud, a good healer who taught me well.'

Black Hawk looked at his brother. 'Our mother spoke of a healer called Sacred Cloud and her sister Two Moons.'

'That's right,' said White Crow. 'Mother said they left her tribe some time before she did, when she became the wife of our father. They were greatly missed . . .'

Blue Bird stared at the two brothers. Her face had suddenly lost all its colour.

Wild Horse knelt beside her. 'What's wrong, Blue Bird?'

'My mother . . .' she said. 'Two Moons was my mother.'

'You never told me your mother's name,' Wild Horse almost whispered, realising he'd never asked.

'For too long it was a name I could not say. Mogoll would not allow it, would not even allow us to talk about her.' She gazed at the black root, as if in a daze. 'I must take this. Thank you.'

Wild Horse watched Blue Bird disappear into Red River's shelter, and waited until she crawled out, her face still the colour of stone. *Now was not the time to talk about Two Moons.* He would wait for her to speak of her mother.

'How is he?' But Wild Horse guessed the answer from

the sadness in her eyes.

Blue Bird cried, 'There is ever more pus, and he has a fever. Even with the black root I cannot heal him. Red River is slipping away.'

The tears flowed down her cheeks as Wild Horse wrapped his arms around her,

'I'm sorry, Blue Bird. Is there no hope?'

'No. He is waiting for the Spirits. He asks for you.'

Wild Horse knelt beside Red River, listened to the broken breathing. 'Well, Red River,' he said, 'it looks like you're going to meet the Spirits with an even better scar than I have, to show what a brave hunter you are.'

Red River tried to smile. 'I didn't kill it . . . so not as good . . . as you.'

'Braver though,' said Wild Horse. 'You saved your sister's life.'

'Thank . . . you . . .' Red River's breathing was heavy. 'Promise me . . . before I go . . . to meet the Spirits . . .'

Wild Horse leant close to catch the hunter's last words.

The shaman's wail grew louder and louder, and when the hunters carried Red River's body to a resting place deep in the forest, it seemed to Wild Horse that it filled the air.

CHAPTER FORTY-ONE

BLUE BIRD

Swift asked Blue Bird to move into the shelter she shared with Red Deer and the two younger sisters, so that they could mourn together, share memories of Red River, leaving Wild Horse alone in his shelter.

Blue Bird felt her insides had been wrenched out, leaving her body drained by the loss of Red River. And of Storm. Sleep did not come easily as night after night she wrestled with everything that had happened.

Some nights later the moon was full and round as she carved a sixth notch in her stick. Everyone else was asleep, but it was warm and she sat outside the shelter gazing at the stars, hoping for guidance.

With Red River gone, was it time to take up the journey to find her mother's family? Her thoughts turned to Black Hawk and White Crow. She hadn't spoken to them since they brought her the black root, yet they knew of her mother and Sacred Cloud. Maybe they could help her find her family. As Storm had found hers. But what of Swift, Little Lion and Feather who had become like sisters to her? Would it be right to leave them?

The sun was not quite awake as she started walking, Paska by her side. She breathed in the dewy freshness, needing to find light beyond her gloom, to start thinking about what lay ahead of her.

Early rays of sun cast shafts of light between the trees as she wandered deeper into the forest. It felt good to be on her own, the first time since Red River had died. She allowed the sounds of the forest to swallow up the sorrow: the chatter of birds and the rustle of leaves. It was right that she let her grief fly into the forest, for the forest was where Red River had belonged.

So deep were her thoughts she hadn't realised how far she'd gone, when a sudden noise startled her – Paska snarled ...

Has my grief made me forget my hunting instinct? That is no way to honour the memory of Red River.

In that instant she realised she wasn't holding a spear.

And she felt hands grabbing her neck.

She whirled, choking, her heart thudding, but the grip

held firm.

'The Spirits have answered my plea and brought you to me.'

Zuni, his eyes flashing like a forest fire.

'I knew I'd find you.'

Paska leapt at him, but he held Blue Bird tightly with one arm and slashed at the dog with his spear. The point caught Paska's ear and she howled.

'This creature has hurt me once, but it won't live to do that again,' he hissed as he pulled his arm back to throw his spear

Terror seized Blue Bird, and with her head pounding and her body shuddering, she yelled, 'Run, Paska! Run-run-run!'

CHAPTER
FORTY-TWO

WILD HORSE

Another nightmare where Zuni dragged Blue Bird away jolted Wild Horse awake. He hadn't dreamt it for some time. As he shook his head to be rid of it, Paska burst into his shelter, barking furiously. Her ear was bleeding.

Wild Horse dashed out of the shelter, expecting to see Blue Bird – was she injured too? – but there was no sign of her. Paska ran round and round, dashing in and out of the trees, still barking.

He ran through the camp, calling her name, and tribespeople sleepily emerged from their shelters, confused by the shouting and barking.

Blue Bird was nowhere to be found.

Bald Eagle said, 'Do you think she's fallen somewhere or been injured?'

'Yes,' said Wild Horse, not daring to think of what had happened in his nightmare, 'and I think she sent Paska back here for help. The dog keeps running back to the trees.'

'Surely Blue Bird wouldn't go into the forest on her own.' Bald Eagle grabbed his spears. 'She knows there are wolves and many other predators there.'

Wild Horse took hold of Paska and looked at the dog's ear. It was no ragged tear. 'It might not be an animal,' he said, his insides twisting like a tornado. 'Paska's ear is cut from the sharp edge of a spear-point. I fear Blue Bird has been taken.'

'What do you mean – *taken*?' asked Black Hawk.

'By my cousin Zuni.'

'Why would your cousin take Blue Bird?' Bald Eagle frowned deeply at Wild Horse.

Wild Horse sighed. It suddenly seemed wrong that they hadn't warned the tribe of the possible peril.

'There is something I regret not telling you, Bald Eagle,' he said, 'but there isn't time to tell you now. I must hurry and follow Paska. She'll lead me to Blue Bird.'

'You mean *us*.' Bald Eagle stepped towards him. 'If Blue Bird is in danger you must not go on your own.'

'I already have much shame that it is my cousin who

threatens Blue Bird. I do not want any of you to risk harm.'

'That is not for you to decide,' said Bald Eagle. 'We will help you find her and bring her back.'

There was no time to argue.

Paska chased into the forest with the hunters behind her. When Paska slowed, Wild Horse knew she was picking up Blue Bird's scent. He took hold of the dog's scruff, to make sure she didn't bound forwards and announce their arrival to Zuni.

If it *was* Zuni.

But something deep inside told Wild Horse that it had to be his cousin. Possibly with the same five hunters. *Six of them against six of us*, he thought, *but Zuni's hunters are older and more experienced. Apart from Dark Wolf . . . Was he still with them?*

They crept forward, Paska pulling at Wild Horse's arm. And then they heard voices, one louder than the others: Zuni's voice.

Wild Horse whispered, 'Let me go ahead. Zuni will think that Blue Bird and I travel alone. Stay close behind, but out of sight until you can see how many there are. You can surround them and then surprise them.'

Bald Eagle said, 'My people have always been peaceful, and there has been no blood of men on my hands, but if the Spirits say blood must be spilled to save Blue Bird, it will be done. The Spirits go with you, Wild Horse.'

Wild Horse asked him to take hold of Paska, and he edged forward, trying to keep his breath soft and even, though he wanted to scream and charge at Zuni. He saw the clearing ahead, saw Blue Bird struggling against sinew ties binding her to a tree. Falcon and three hunters sat on felled trees, talking quietly. There was no sign of Dark Wolf. Zuni strutted round Blue Bird, threatening her with his spear.

'I thought that wretched dog might bring my cowardly cur of a cousin to rescue you.' He pressed his spear-point close to Blue Bird's neck. 'But it seems he doesn't have the courage.'

'I haven't seen Wild Horse for many moons,' said Blue Bird. 'We agreed we had different paths to follow.'

Zuni peered into Blue Bird's eyes, 'Why should I believe you?'

'You don't have to believe me, but why else would you find me alone in the forest with Paska?'

'Dark Wolf.' Zuni snorted.

'Who is Dark Wolf?' she said.

'My brother. It makes sense. He released Wild Horse, then disappeared. They must have run off together, probably back to Bear Face. Cowards.'

'You're wrong – Wild Horse is no coward,' said Blue Bird.

'Well he's not here protecting you, is he? Now to decide whether I return you to Mogoll alive, or take my revenge for the way you left me to die by the river . . .'

Blue Bird shrank away from the spear, but her eyes flashed. 'These are Mogoll's hunters. They might be glad to see me returned to my father, but they would not see me killed by your hand. Would you?' She glared at the hunters. 'Falcon, you've known me all my life. Would you let me be harmed?'

Wild Horse saw Falcon look away.

'They are here with me, not Mogoll.' Zuni lowered his spear as he leant close to her, his mouth almost touching her ear.

Wild Horse couldn't bear to watch any more.

'Get away from her!'

He leapt into the clearing and was on Zuni in a moment, punching him to the ground with a ferocity he didn't know he had.

'You talk of courage, but *you* are the coward who ties a girl to a tree.' The hunters jumped to their feet as Wild Horse spun round shouting, 'You call yourselves hunters. But you're *all* cowards. You bring no honour to Mogoll treating his daughter like this.'

The hunters looked shocked at his words, but Zuni staggered up and ran at Wild Horse with all his might. The two cousins fought with fists and fury on the forest floor, their spears forgotten. So much bitterness surging out of them. So much anger after being rivals for so long.

Bald Eagle's hunters ran into the clearing with Paska barking loudly. In that moment Zuni looked up, startled, and Wild Horse swung his clenched fist into Zuni's jaw. Zuni fell to the ground, stunned, his eyes rolling back. Wild Horse heard Bald Eagle shouting at Mogoll's hunters to lay down their spears and no harm would come to them.

They didn't seem to put up a fight, which Wild Horse

thought they could have. They were probably stronger than Bald Eagle's hunters, even though they were outnumbered.

Wild Horse ran to free Blue Bird, slicing through her bonds with his stone knife.

She grinned at him and patted Paska. 'I knew she'd go and get you.'

'She did well. And so did you – standing up to Zuni. And you really shamed Falcon. Are you all right? Did Zuni hurt you?'

'Not as much as I hurt him when I bit his arm!' she replied.

A scream made them both spin round.

Black Hawk lay on the ground, clutching his arm. White Crow knelt next to him.

And Zuni had gone.

'I'm sorry!' Black Hawk cried. 'He seemed too badly injured to get up, but as I leant over him he slashed at me with his spear, Wild Horse – I'm sorry, I was a fool.'

'No, you weren't,' said Wild Horse. 'Zuni is a snake – deceiving people is what he does best.'

'I'll go after him,' said White Crow. 'Make him pay for what he has done to Blue Bird and Black Hawk.'

'No.' Wild Horse grabbed his spears. 'You look after your brother. Zuni is *mine*. It's just me now.'

'And me.' Blue Bird stood next to Wild Horse, Paska at her side. 'And Paska. The three of us.'

'It's not a job for a girl,' said White Crow. 'I should go with Wild Horse.'

Wild Horse took a deep breath and smiled at his friend. 'Blue Bird is not just a girl,' he said, passing her one of his spears. 'She is a hunter!'

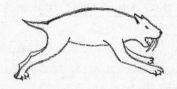

CHAPTER
FORTY-THREE

WILD HORSE

Wild Horse's head throbbed as he hurtled out of the clearing – thoughts of Zuni circling round and round. He couldn't let him get away. Not this time. He kept his eyes fixed to the forest floor, looking for any signs of Zuni's route – newly broken twigs, trodden down leaves . . .

'Paska!' Blue Bird called the dog to sniff the neckline of her tunic. 'Find!'

The dog plunged through the undergrowth and into the dense forest.

'Quick, Wild Horse. Paska has picked up his scent.'

'How?'

'Zuni grabbed me round the throat. He left his scent.'

Wild Horse raced after the dog, the thought of Zuni grabbing Blue Bird round the throat making him almost sick with rage.

A herd of deer thundered towards them, fleeing between the trees, not knowing that for once the hunter's spear would not follow them. Wild Horse cursed that they had to wait for the herd to pass. He feared that whatever had startled them might cover Zuni's scent.

Paska slowed, sniffing the ground, trying to find the trail. Frustration coursed through Wild Horse – then he paused as he heard the distant sound of water gushing over rocks. The waterfall of the Falling River lay ahead of them.

'That's it,' he said. 'It was Zuni who frightened the deer towards us. He must've disturbed them while they were drinking at the river.'

He started running towards the sounds of the water, Blue Bird and Paska close behind. As he came to the edge of the forest he slowed, darting from tree to tree, to keep out of sight.

And yes – there was Zuni, wading across the river, fighting the current which splashed round his thighs as the water swirled round rocks that jutted out of the surface.

The Falling River was deeper here as it rushed towards the waterfall. Zuni slipped and lost his footing, but he grabbed a rock and held on, before he set off again. He was heading towards a rough low cliff on the opposite riverbank, but was too far away for Wild Horse's spear to reach.

Wild Horse felt desperate. On the other side of the river was more forest where Zuni could soon disappear. If only the deer hadn't slowed them down and given his cousin the advantage . . .

Sudden movement at the top of the cliff caught his attention.

'Look, Blue Bird . . .' he whispered, and she nodded. She'd already seen it.

A herd of mammoth: seven adults and three calves. The smallest was already the size of a bison. They were moving quickly out of the trees and towards the cliff edge.

Zuni was looking down at the rocks beneath the surface of the rushing water, trying to get a good foothold.

'I don't think Zuni has seen them,' said Blue Bird softly.

'And they haven't seen Zuni . . .'

Wild Horse didn't dare move. If the mammoths saw him, they might turn away from the river, and he needed them to stampede into it, to drive Zuni back.

'Wild Horse . . .' Blue Bird pointed.

A shadow slinking out from the trees behind the mammoths. It was a sabretooth cat, scrawny and hungry: that was why the mammoths were in a hurry. Its eyes were firmly on the baby mammoth on the edge of the herd.

'Blue Bird,' muttered Wild Horse, 'see how the cat moves . . .'

'How she lowers her head and gazes at her prey,' Blue Bird finished.

'Storm . . .'

'I can't believe it,' said Blue Bird. 'She lives.'

'And now she is our best hope.'

Blue Bird frowned. 'How?'

'If she remembers my signals she can stampede the mammoths towards Zuni and he'll have to turn back to this side of the river.'

Wild Horse raised his arm slowly, so as not to alarm the mammoths. The sabretooth was focused on the baby mammoth, but as Wild Horse curled his fingers, just a small motion, it caught the cat's eye and she looked up and stared at him, ears pricked, nose in the air.

'It's me, Storm,' Wild Horse whispered into the rush off the river, willing her to catch his scent, to know it was him, as he knew her.

She cocked her head. Zuni was pushing his way through the water again, drawing closer to the riverbank. Wild Horse had to be quick now, and Storm had to remember him and react to the signals he'd taught her. Blue Bird and Paska were silent, as if they knew this was Wild Horse's fight.

As Wild Horse moved his hand back and forth, Storm began to move too – to run back and forth, forcing the mammoths down the cliff. They began to panic and bellow.

Zuni looked up and froze where he stood, the water rushing around him.

Wild Horse signalled to Storm to charge at the herd and as she did, so the animals stampeded down the cliff and into the water. Zuni turned and started to come back, but then he saw Wild Horse waiting for him on the riverbank.

Wild Horse stepped forward. He fastened his gaze on Zuni and held up his spear. This time he was in control and Zuni was the one in danger.

'You've got two choices, Zuni,' he shouted. 'Take your chance against the mammoths, or prove you are the brave hunter and come back to this side of the river to fight me one against one.'

'You're not worthy of a fight.' Zuni's face twisted with bitterness. 'I'll take my chances.' And he turned his back on Wild Horse.

Storm was still pushing the mammoths towards Zuni, and Wild Horse felt sure his cousin would turn back when he realised the mammoths were blocking his escape.

But Zuni started wading downriver, towards the waterfall.

Wild Horse splashed into the river, cursing into the din of the mammoths bawling as they heaved through the surging water. The baby mammoth, shrieking in terror, lurched forwards and fell into the fast flow. It tried to get a foothold, but its body was tossed forward and from that moment, everything happened so quickly.

The baby crashed into Zuni, knocking him off his feet and into the water.

All Wild Horse could hear were Zuni's screams as he and the baby mammoth plunged over the edge of the waterfall.

Wild Horse stood in the river, gazing at the space where

Zuni had been. It was as if everything else had stopped. In spite of the noise around him, he couldn't hear anything or see anything – there was just emptiness.

And then a noise, a shout, seeped through.

'Wild Horse,' Blue Bird yelled. 'Look out!'

He turned. The matriarch of the herd was very close to him – snorting and stamping, her trunk swinging wildly. She could easily charge and tip him over the waterfall too.

And suddenly Wild Horse was back beside another river, all those moons ago, facing the young bull mammoth on his own. It seemed so long ago.

He held out his arms, tried to remember what he'd said and spoke the words again: *'We have both shown courage.'*

He kept his eyes fixed on the mammoth.

'I am sorry for the loss of your baby. I meant you no harm.'

The matriarch kept swinging her huge trunk as if to swipe Wild Horse away.

'Lead your herd to safety,' said Wild Horse, breathing deeply and calmly, though he felt anything but calm. *'Let us both live this day that we might meet another.'*

A booming wail filled the air as the huge beast stepped towards Wild Horse, then slowly – time seemed to move so slowly now – turned from Wild Horse . . . Wild Horse watched the herd leave the river. He shook his head, trying to make sense of everything that had just happened. A mix of disbelief and relief, of joy and anguish poured through him. It wasn't the end he'd wanted for Zuni. Or was it?

He watched Storm prowl along the water's edge, her nose in the air, before she headed for the rocks on the far side of the waterfall. He thought he saw a glimpse of other cat-like shadows shifting in the trees beyond.

Blue Bird called again, and he turned to see her and Paska running along the near riverbank. When he turned back, Storm and the shadows were gone.

CHAPTER FORTY-FOUR

BLUE BIRD

Blue Bird could hardly believe what she'd seen. Zuni was dead, and Storm was alive.

'Wild Horse, you did it!' She grabbed him and hugged him as he came out of the water.

'Storm did it.' He pulled back, looked across to the other side of the river.

'What's wrong? It is a good day. The Spirits blessed us.'

'It just all happened so suddenly and I can't believe Zuni's gone.'

'Well, he is, and Storm is back.' Blue Bird gazed into the

forest. 'Where is she? I want to see her, to stroke her.'

'She's been living in the wild, Blue Bird. She might have recognised us, but she is wild now. She looked hungry. I think she climbed down the far side of the waterfall. It looked like she'd picked up the scent of the mammoth baby . . . or Zuni.'

'Oh. Yes,' Blue Bird shuddered. A small part of her wanted the cub to swim towards her and rub her shoulder against Blue Bird's leg, like she used to.

'That's what I should do. I should find Zuni's body. He is my kin, and you said that even Zuni has a soul.'

'I did,' she said.

Bald Eagle and his hunters strode towards them through the trees. 'We watched your stand, Wild Horse – it was very brave. You showed great understanding of animals. And I am glad you have defeated your enemy.'

He grasped Wild Horse's shoulder. 'The Spirits were with you, my son. They didn't want you to have the blood of your kin on your hands. They let you use your skills and knowledge of animals against him, rather than your spear. It is a better end.'

'What you say is wise,' said Wild Horse. 'And now I must collect Zuni's body, so that his spirit might be set free.'

Blue Bird stayed with Bald Eagle and Black Hawk as Wild Horse led the hunters down the rocks, to the base of the waterfall.

'How are you, Black Hawk?' she asked. That he'd shown such courage against Zuni had touched her.

'The bleeding has stopped,' he said. 'The cut isn't too deep.'

She reached for the balm in her pouch. 'I'll spread a little of this on it. It will heal better.' She turned to Bald Eagle. 'What happened to Mogoll's hunters?'

'I told them I did not want their blood on my hands,' said the chief. 'There are enough dangers to face from the animals and the forces of nature, that the people who walk the earth should not fight amongst themselves.'

'They are lucky you are such a wise chief,' she said. 'So you let them go?'

'They did not like the way the kin of Wild Horse had treated you. I told them to tell Mogoll that he brought shame to their tribe by such actions. That he was not worthy of having the daughter of a chief for his wife. They agreed.'

Blue Bird smiled. 'I hope my father doesn't send anybody else to take me back when he finds out where I am.'

Bald Eagle shook his head. 'I do not think he will. I gave them one last message for Mogoll – that there should be freedom between tribes, and that you had become a daughter of our tribe.' He put his arm round her shoulder. 'I look on you as a daughter, but if you decide you wish to return to your father's tribe, we will take you there in peace.'

Blue Bird smiled at the chief. 'I left my father's tribe to find my mother's family, but it seems I've found this family instead.'

'Blue Bird . . .' said Black Hawk hesitating, 'there is something else that White Crow and I need to tell you . . .'

CHAPTER
FORTY-FIVE

WILD HORSE

There was no sign of either Zuni or the baby mammoth at the bottom of the waterfall.

'Their bodies must have been washed away in the rapids,' said Hook Nose. 'Nothing could have survived the fall on to those rocks.'

'He's right,' said White Crow. 'If a baby mammoth couldn't survive the force of the undercurrent, then neither could a hunter.'

Wild Horse knew what they said must be true, but he wanted the proof of a body. He insisted the hunters walk along the riverbank, but all they found was one of Zuni's spears lodged between two rocks. A low growl floated across the river from the forest on the other side, shadows skulking then gone. A sabretooth pack could have dragged both bodies out of the river into the cover of the forest . . .

Wild Horse stood there a long time before he knew it was time to leave.

Back at the camp, Bald Eagle said to him, 'Zuni got the end he deserved. The Spirits decided a watery resting place was the best one for such a restless damaged soul.'

'Yes,' agreed Wild Horse.

'I've talked to the hunters, and the rest of the tribe, and they all agree that you must stay and take Red River's place as lead hunter.'

Wild Horse gulped back his surprise. 'I feel happy here – and it would be an honour to lead the hunters. But it is the way that one of *your* people should lead. What about Water Snake? He is your brother, so it should pass to him. Or Hook Nose? Red River told me he was his best hunter. I do not wish to dishonour them.'

'You will not dishonour them, Wild Horse. You are the one they trust and wish to follow,' said Bald Eagle. 'The way of *our* people is that our hunters choose their leader. They chose Red River and now they choose you.' He went on, 'And *you* should speak of us as "*our* people", not "*your* people". You belong with us.'

'Thank you. That is kind.'

'It is not kind,' said the chief. 'It is the truth. I speak what we all believe.'

*

'So much has happened since I wandered through the trees at first light,' Blue Bird said as they sat by the campfire that night. 'Beginnings and endings.'

'The end of Zuni, you mean?' said Wild Horse.

'Yes, but there's another ending as well.'

'What's that?'

'Well, it's an ending *and* a beginning.' She was holding her notched stick and her face glowed in the light of the fire.

'Are you going to tell me what that is?' he asked.

She passed the stick to Wild Horse. 'I no longer yearn to be the son my father wanted. I am Blue Bird. And Bald Eagle thinks of me as a daughter of this tribe.'

Wild Horse said, 'I feel the same. It doesn't matter what Bear Face thinks of me now – I *know* that I've proved myself, that I'm not my brother. And if Dark Wolf has returned to my father's tribe as he wanted to, he can be the lead hunter. My brother Grey Horse can become Chief when it's Bear Face's time to meet the Spirits. Bald Eagle has asked me to lead the hunters here – it is as Tall Tree told me. I think he would be proud.'

'And so would Running Bear,' said Blue Bird. 'It's a new beginning for both of us.'

'And the stick?' Wild Horse closed his hand round it.

'At the start of our journey I carved the stick and decided I'd make a notch for each moon it took me to find my mother's family. There are six notches.'

'But you haven't found your mother's family.'

Blue Bird grinned. 'I have, Wild Horse. Black Hawk and White Crow tell me that the fathers of my mother and their mother were brothers. We're cousins. They are my family.'

'That is good, Blue Bird. I'm pleased for you.'

'Thank you. But I haven't just found cousins. I've got three new sisters – and a new brother.'

'New brother?'

'You, Wild Horse. You are like a brother to me. I hope you can look on me as a sister.'

Wild Horse smiled. 'It will be an honour,' he said. 'And I'll look after you always.'

As Red River had asked him to do. It was an easy promise to make – and easier still to keep.

Blue Bird squeezed Wild Horse's hand around the stick and then traced the outline of a star on his forehead. 'And as the new leader of the hunters I hope you will allow your sister to hunt with you,' she grinned.

'By my side,' said Wild Horse, grinning back. 'Like a brother.'

AUTHOR'S ACKNOWLEDGEMENTS AND NOTES

First, thanks to The Times Chicken House judges for awarding me first prize of publication for the 2013 Children's Fiction Competition. In particular to Barry Cunningham whose words 'I really like your book' are imprinted in my brain. Mind you, he didn't tell me how much editing there was to do, but to this end I am grateful to Rachel Leyshon, whose editing skills kept me going. It's true; perseverance pays. And of course thanks to everyone else at Chicken House.

Personal thanks go to Peter, an extraordinary lover of all things historical, who introduced me to the Clovis culture, and who avidly read my early efforts; and to my other reader, my sister Gaye, for her support and encouragement. And to Lola my labradoodle, who accompanies me on my daily walks, where I gather thoughts for the day's writing.

Although this story is of course fictional I loved diving into the research. The internet was invaluable, but I must also mention a fascinating book by Gary Haynes: *The Early Settlement of North America, The Clovis Era*.

But there is comparatively little known about the Clovis hunter gatherers who lived in North America 13,000 years ago towards the end of the Pleistocene epoch. Major ecological changes were occurring, such as drought in some areas, which reduced the number of water sources for both humans and animals.

The Clovis Paleo-Indians are so named because the site of the first discovery of their distinctive fluted spear-point was Clovis, New Mexico in 1932. More were found across much of North America – the largest were about 4cm wide (and 14cm long!)

Language would have been limited, so the Clovis may not have had specific terms for the seasons, but they would have been aware of changing weather patterns – the winter periods of long cold nights contrasted with longer warmer days – and of regular changes in the moon, hence Blue Bird making notches in her stick.

I had fun sketching the chapter heading illustrations; although there is no known Clovis cave art – a mammoth bone carved with an image of a mammoth was once found in Florida. And I enjoyed inventing clothes for my characters with variations of Native American clothing. The breechcloth is simply a length of hide draped between the legs and flapped over a belt at front and back.

The journey of Blue Bird and Wild Horse takes place across modern-day Texas, as shown on the map, using some real locations: so the Enchanted Rock becomes the Sacred Rock, the Mississippi River is the Great River, and the Arkansas River is the Falling River. The mountain range on the west of the map is the Rockies. The Clovis hunted megamammals, all of which became extinct about the same time that the Clovis people were superseded by a people called the Folsom. It's argued that the Clovis caused the extinction, or at least greatly contributed to it, by over-killing, but the rapid climate change is also likely to have been a factor. The animals they hunted include:

*Smilodon/*sabretoothed cat (also wrongly called the sabretoothed *tiger*). Standing at up to 1.4 m at the shoulder, the sabretooth is best known for its long canine teeth which could protrude out of the upper jaw by as much as 16 cm.

*Mammuthus/*mammoth or hairy mammoth. With a pronounced hump on its back and a body length up to 3.5 m the mammoth is recognised by its long curved tusks which would be as long the body if they weren't so curved. Preferred grazing on open grassland, though could survive in woodland.

*Mammut/*mastodon. Similar size to the mammoth, also with thick hairy outer coat, but its tusks were shorter, 1.5 m (and less curved). Unlike the mammoth, it preferred to eat leaves and plants, so was found in forests and wooded areas. Both needed to forage for food between water sources. In arid times they could dig for waterholes with their hooves.

Arctodus simus/short-faced bear. On all fours the adult male stood up to 1.8 m at shoulder height, but upright stood at 4 m. A hefty predator built for endurance rather than speed, but could use its bulk to threaten lesser predators away from their kill.

Megatherium/giant sloth. On the ground this beast stood as large as a mammoth, but often used its broad muscular tail for support to stand on its hind legs, when it reached up to 6 m. Used its huge claws, up to 30 cm long, to grab leaves. Although mainly a herbivore it may have scavenged from the dead prey of other animals.

Canis dirus/dire wolf, about 1.5 m/5 ft long with long pointed teeth. Hunted in packs.

And as you'll see in this approximate scale sketch, they would all have been absolutely terrifying!

Mastodon   Giant sloth   Sabretooth   Short-faced
                                cat   bear

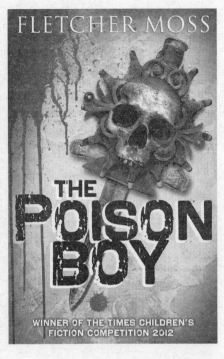

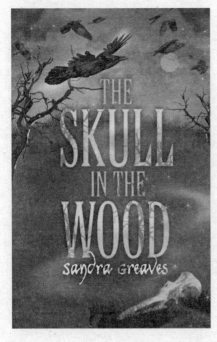